Mighty Men
RISING

MIGHTY MEN RISING

K.C. Lindberg

XULON PRESS

Xulon Press
2301 Lucien Way #415
Maitland, FL 32751
407.339.4217
www.xulonpress.com

xulon
PRESS

Paperback ISBN-13: 978-1-66282-667-2
Ebook ISBN-13: 978-1-66282-668-9

PROLOGUE

Nightmare, Tanya Anderson's Apartment

I woke with a strangled cry, legs tangled in my sheets from twisting and turning of my nightmare. Struggling with my breathing, my imagination reminding me of the smoke burning in my lungs; recalling the terror of lying in the debris, unable to hear those around me who were obviously shouting.

I pushed my way to a sitting position in my bed and brushed my hair from my face, feeling tears running down my cheeks. Why, after so many weeks, did I still have this reoccurring nightmare?

The memories flooded back. I recalled my horror when I first saw the flames leaping high in the sky, a hellish scene against the dark night. My fear escalating because I didn't understand what had happened and I couldn't find my cameraman. Failure loomed in my mind realizing I was experiencing something big as a reporter and didn't yet have a clue what it could be.

After 'speaking' though an impromptu combination of sign language and smoke induced hoarseness with several police officers and firemen, a frantic search for my cameraman began. The hunt came to an end as they discovered my seriously injured partner in the temporary triage area. It was at that moment the full weight of reality fell upon me.

The fateful whispered words uttered by my cameraman about seeing two figures running away, motivated everyone to search for his camera. I was plunged into the worst week of my life, the week the world seemed to turn upside down. I had experienced firsthand a terrorist attack that would haunt me for the rest of my life.

I recalled my embarrassment as I learned of the multiple brutal attacks carried out against the U.S. on October 10th. The Silver Springs, Maryland school hostage situation ended with three dead Americans, followed by the Chicago Mercantile Exchange attack, where I was reporting, with at least fifteen dead with several Board members still hospitalized. The anguish of the day had moved into higher gear as the nation learned of the various suicide bombing attempts in Las Vegas, followed by an explosion at Boulder Dam. These attacks, believed to have been done by terrorists already in the country, had left scores of people dead and injured, and caused damages now estimated in the billions of dollars. When the actuality of the whole day became clear, a nation stood again changed and angry, scared and ready to fight.

Having been on scene during one of the attacks, I, Tanya Anderson, became the face of the news. Although it was great for my career, I was interviewed until I was ready to crawl into a cave. But, in the midst of this negativity, I was ashamed to admit to myself that the tall officer who had strode into my office with his deep chocolate brown eyes, short brown hair, perfectly tanned skin and erect carriage, held a prominent place in my thoughts. The man whose piercing eyes had seemed to touch me down to my soul continued to linger in my mind, even though we personally had rarely even spoken to each other. His associate, equally fit and striking had been the first to interview me, leaving me with a strong sense of relief that my preparation for that meeting had been as detailed as possible. The other man, whose name I vaguely remembered as Christian, had asked such penetrating questions, that it helped me be totally prepared for all the other interviews to come. He had forced my thoughts to be precise and consistent. But it was the tall man, whose name I had learned later to be John Banks, who stuck in my mind, my visceral reaction to him an entirely new experience.

CHAPTER 1

Black Friday Death and Chaos

In the early morning traffic, still dark and cold, an old grayish cargo van sputtered down I-20 in Atlanta, aggravating the rushing shoppers with its slow speed. Focused on their rush to the shopping areas, no one took any notice of the vehicle except to admonish the driver with hand gestures. As the van neared the Capital Street overpass, it veered sharply to the left causing lots of brakes to scream and horns to blast. Pulling under the overpass onto the grassy shoulder between the north and south interstate lanes, the driver jumped out of the cargo van in this safe area. He went to the front of his vehicle and raised the hood to stare at the engine, reaching in his pocket and pulling out the container of water, he stealthily set it up to drip on the hot engine, creating a misty smoke wafting upward.

After watching the smoke for a few moments, a car pulled up and the van driver jumped in and they sped off leaving the smoking cargo van sitting with its hood raised. It was safe for a time since the raised hood indicated a problem and passing traffic ignored it as it was a common sight on I-20. It was 7:36 AM and traffic was heavy with Black Friday shoppers hurrying from one shopping area to another. Folks were always up early on the day after Thanksgiving trying to get all the best deals.

Traffic reached the height of madness when the cargo van suddenly exploded in a rush of heat, force, and flames pushing the cars nearest it skidding across the lanes. Debris falling from the mangled under-structure of the Capital Street overpass first peppered the cars in the north bound lanes of I-20, and then bigger chunks of concrete fell onto the road causing a screeching halt to movement, multiple rear end crashes creating a domino effect down the high-speed interstate. One lady called 911 from her cell and sank back against her car seat.

Above on the overpass, bewildered drivers felt the force hit and quickly realized their danger. Spotting rapidly expanding cracks in the road from the weakened structure, the scene devolved into crashing cars, frightened and sometimes bloody people jumping from their vehicles. More folks called 911 on their cell phones.

The Fulton County Sheriff's Department (FCSD) reaction was swift as they were close and the main Atlanta Police Station was also near enough to respond in minutes. The scene before them encompassed their greatest nightmare. Cars lay in heaps, smoking and crumpled against one another. First responders reaching Capital Street above found a similar mess to deal with. People were hysterical, shouting or quiet, too quiet. FCSD Patrol Officers began to direct traffic to the side as ambulances quickly began to arrive. As FCSD were accessing the main problems to be dealt with, a media van emblazoned with WTBS arrived on the side street of Pryor. Officers groaned but stuck to their tasks. So far, they could not verify that anyone had died and the worst injuries seemed confined to the tangled mess of former vehicles shoved together across several lanes by the blast. It would take several hours to clear it all and get the people trapped in the steaming mass of metal out. Fire trucks arrived to evaluate the best way to safely approach the smoking mess.

A lady reporter, Julia Carmichael, from the media van soon approached the Sheriff to ask the usual questions, camera rolling. He bit off a bitter reply and answered shortly, "we have no answers yet and I must ask you to stay back. There is still a chance of further problems from leaking fuel or from falling debris. Our first priority is to get the injured out of danger and to the hospital for evaluation. Take whatever pictures you want but from a safe distance. I can't be worried about you being inj...."

Julia gasped as she noticed a red dot appear in the sheriff's head, an instant later a crack resounded from behind her and the Sheriff slumped to the ground, a small hole in his forehead.

Taking one horrified step back, she turned slightly to see her astute cameraman swing his camera 180 degrees to scan the tall buildings and area behind her. He focused in as tight as was possible from his standpoint and then scanned back and forth. His hope was to catch any suspicious movement from that direction. The shooter must be within his range.

After a moment of stunned stillness, the entire place erupted into chaotic action by the police, sheriffs and EMTs. The closest EMT a former Army medic tackled the reporter and cameraman, yelling stay down, and then crawled to the Sheriff only to shake his head, no. The bullet had been straight into the forehead causing immediate death. The EMT covered the Sheriff's head with a coat in order to deal with him later, the living taking precedence over the dead.

The rest of the EMTs and Law Enforcement personnel crouched behind cars looking for the gunman or stayed low as they moved toward wrecked cars to help the trapped passengers. The lead investigator immediately ordered a perimeter established around the entire scene, expecting possible additional shots. All the agencies there immediately placed calls for backup.

Julia lay in silent shock until her cameraman nudged her after he had finished his scans. Shaking herself, she began to gather her thoughts on how to report this in a news bulletin. Her thoughts bounced around in her head, shocked by the first murder she had seen. How could she possibly say what had happened on air? Only then, as she scanned herself for the interview, did she notice the blood spattered on her clothes. She shivered but remembered the reporter from Chicago who had bravely stood to speak on camera in tattered and dirty clothes, with a voice husky with smoke, in the aftermath of the bombing there.

"O, Lord," she thought, "could this be another attack? What to say, how to say it cluttered her thoughts because she'd repeatedly been warned not to say things that could cause panic in the city. But what could she say that would not cause panic for the people of Atlanta? A vehicle blowing up on the busy interstate during the Black Friday rush followed by the killing of the FCSD Sheriff during the response, could only be another attack, right? Was it beginning again?" Wishing for a moment to talk with her editor for some welcome direction, she none the less, shook herself and spoke into the camera with as calm a voice she could muster, telling the people of her city just what she had just witnessed.

The Atlanta Police Department (APD) Chief arrived to take over command, mourning the loss of his friend but determined that this would not escalate or destroy his city as the Olympic bombings at Centennial Park during the summer games in 1996 nearly had. He stood still as his men and the sheriff deputies gave him a quick but certainly incomplete up-date. Things were moving too fast for anyone to have a comprehensive explanation for the terrible event. His thoughts kept returning to the Olympic mess, and the totally unexplained events of 10/10 last month. He began to wonder if all hell had broken loose in his nation. He forced himself to focus on what his men were telling him.

"Sir," the first officer on the scene caught his attention, "the best we can tell right now is that a vehicle parked beneath the overpass went up in flames suddenly exploded, causing a blast wave that knocked cars sideways on both sides of the interstate, mostly on the south bound side. The second major problem is that the road above was damaged and debris began falling on the vehicle's underneath. All this triggered massive pile-ups above and below. We're trying to assess the injured now. Fire is working on using the 'jaws of life' to extricate people from their cars but they are hampered by the steam and possible explosions from damaged gas tanks. We are cautioning all the workers to be aware of that potential. It has hampered any real understanding of how many and how badly people are hurt, and we don't want to rush too much and cause any victims or responders to be hurt by fire or explosions. The shot that killed Sheriff McGee seems to have come from the direction to the east of the interstate and the FCSD have teams checking all the buildings in the general line of fire. But, Sir, this will take time. There are dozens of tall buildings that the shooter could have used and we have to clear each of them in hopes of finding anything definitive. I guess that about covers where we are right now, Sir."

The Police Chief nodded his understanding and tersely added, "I'm going to call in Homeland Security, the FBI, and extra help from our surrounding area police and sheriff departments. This is big and I want all the bases covered as quickly as possible. I noticed that WTBS has a van on site. Find out if there is any film we can review. Otherwise continue as you have, you have done well so far."

CHAPTER 2

Surveying the Destruction

Christian Blade and I, John Banks, two members of a special task force started by Earnest Trowbridge, the president's Chief of Staff (COS) after the October attacks, arrived at mid-day. Delayed temporarily from our travel to Iowa to see what was up in Atlanta, we contacted the APD Chief of Police and the local FBI agent in charge.

I noticed immediately that the APD Police Chief was harried and a bit abrupt with us until a FBI agent leaned over and whispered that the President's COS had asked him to include the two of us in the investigation. The APD Chief began slowly but started rushing as he spoke.

"It's still touch and go as our first responders try to extricate people from mangled and crushed vehicles, gas spilling onto the pavement or other vehicles. The work is slow as we try to avoid creating sparks and starting any more fires than we are already dealing with. All we know for sure now is that an old cargo van was left with the hood raised under the overpass at Capital Street. We have canvassed as many people as we can talk to but they are all confused and hurting and don't remember seeing the vehicle themselves. We are trying to decide what to broadcast so that anyone who might have seen the vehicle or who left it will contact us. And that's about where we are now. It will take more time to clear all the vehicles, decide what to do about the spilt gas, and the Sherriff. He is, uh, was a friend of mine and I understand that he was killed by a high-powered rifle from somewhere in that direction," he said waving his hand in the general direction of the surrounding buildings to the east.

Having listened carefully, I nodded as the Chief spoke, and I thought of a few questions to ask but also knew that few answers were available at this time. After the Chief stopped talking, a young officer came up to inform the Chief that the area around the van was cool enough now for a closer inspection. I asked, "Would it be ok if Christian and I went with you? Christian is an Explosive Ordinance Disposal (EOD) instructor at Redstone Arsenal where we are stationed."

The Chief just nodded and strode off toward the truck not even noticing whether we followed or not. I noticed the Chief was growing angrier by the moment as the reality of what had happened sunk in. Christian and I, understanding, jogged along with him. As we approached the burned-out hump of metal, Christian nodded. He began a quick circle around it taking in the twisted metal, the smell of explosives, along with the smell of burnt rubber and material, reminiscent of Iraq. Christian scanned the truck, looking for any possible hints. It would be taken in for a full forensic examination but he wanted to gather his own first impressions. As he walked, he noted the charred condition along with massive tearing in the vehicle's sides and top indicating to him that he was observing more than a vehicle that blew up from a simple malfunction. His own experiences in the military caused him to seriously consider a truck bomb. His thoughts grew darker as he considered the implications of that. Convinced in his mind that he was dealing with a probable terrorist attack, he was very glad they had called in Homeland Security along with the FBI.

Christian met the Chief as they each completed their circle of the vehicle. Christian waited a moment and then asked, "What do you think?"

The Chief looked startled, suddenly realizing he wasn't alone. He motioned with his hand, "this looks like more than a 'car trouble' mess. Somebody must have packed this thing with some heavy-duty explosives. I saw some results of IEDs (Improvised Explosive Devices) while in the military but nothing this big. I believe we have a terrorist attack on our hands, plus the murder of the Sherriff. I am glad that someone from the government is here. We have a good forensics team but nothing like the FBI or DHS. I hope you guys can help also. I understand that the President's COS sent you?"

"Yes, Sir, we've been tasked to help in the follow up to the 10/10 attacks but this seems to be a part of it also. We will be following up with all of you and reporting to the authorities." We are an extra set of eyes that go to every attack site and are trying to come up with a common thread. We are trying to keep the existence of our team out of public knowledge."

I watched as the first responders set up lights as the November day grew gray and overcast. I observed the scene as the feverous work of getting the victims out and cared for continued unabated. The influx of additional responders from surrounding metropolitan Atlanta showed up in force and the work took on a practiced precision. Teams worked in each of the several designated areas of concern. First, fire and Rescue along with the EMTs worked to help those trapped in their cars and move them swiftly to area hospitals. Grady Memorial was the closest but even its facilities were quickly overwhelmed and other hospitals were notified to expect casualties. The work was momentous but fell into the practiced ebb and flow of triage. These kinds of events were trained for with the hope that these skills would never be needed.

Because of the care and patient work to avoid extra harm, it was midnight before the injured were all safely in hospitals and the road cleared of vehicles but this main artery through town was still closed. Unfortunately, the Sherriff's death wasn't the only one and the body count was expected to rise since some of the injuries were life threatening, especially those in the closest range of the explosion or those in the lane that were slammed into the concrete wall.

I knew that transportation inspectors would be on scene in the morning to fully evaluate the damages and determine whether they could reopen the roads. I heard the bulletin aired and saw the posted warning on the overhead traffic signs. People cut short their shopping to go home and consider the possibilities of what had happened. I could feel the anger grow all afternoon in this city of Southern charm and high-power business.

Christian and I remained on the scene until all the injured were safely extricated and transported. We had also observed the still smoking pile of metal as it was hauled to the Police compound, where it was already undergoing examination.

So far APD had determined the cargo van had been packed with explosives, presumed to be ammonium nitrate based but had not uncovered the detonator yet. The most interesting find was the video footage from traffic cameras of the van pulling over and then appearing to overheat.

The problem was the footage from the cameras was too far away to get a good look at the driver. This meant it was more than deliberate; it was well planned and skillfully carried out. Everyone's anger just kept mounting.

I informed Trowbridge of these findings and Christian's assessment of the van at the scene. There was no doubt that this was a deliberate attack. The nation had barely recovered from the failed raid at the Iowa compound with the FBI and ATF losing more than 15 men and now this coming on a holiday weekend. It would be a long time in recovery.

Earnest replied, "Homeland Security and the FBI have officially taken over the investigation and I have informed the President that another terrorist attack was a real potential. We advised the nation by the media. We unfortunately stand on the brink of another time of questions and recriminations from all sides."

"You two go on to Iowa, check with me daily and prepare a comprehensive report for our next meeting. We will delay that meeting for about a week in view of the Atlanta event.

CHAPTER 3

Creating the Mighty Men

Huntsville, AL November 9th:

This afternoon, the sky darkening at only 4:00 PM caught my eye from the small window across from my desk. Half of my mind was on the weather that held a promise of thunderstorms, always a concern in the southern states, while the other half was reading another report on the disastrous days of fall. The atrocious attacks of 10/10 and the failed assault by the FBI and ATF on the Iowa-based camp thought to have been instrumental in carrying out those attacks still puzzled me. I felt weighed down by the knowledge that no one had a solid understanding of how, who, or from where such devastation had come.

The terrorists had carried out highly coordinated and skillful attacks on multiple targets across three time zones in the United States that day, wreaking devastation across the nation. It was suspected that they were living in the country in clandestine camps but also as neighbors and coworkers, all the while harboring the underlying intent of attacking their new home in support of their cause. They killed and maimed many, destroyed businesses and even managed to shut down part of the electrical grid on

October 10th. Their actions created a sense of anger that had not been felt since September 11, 2001.

The phone rang, interrupting my thoughts; I answered, Banks, how may I help you?" I was surprised as I recognized the voice on the other end. I really hadn't thought to hear from the Earnest, so soon. Yet I was the contact person for a team of military trained personnel chosen by the President to go to each individual site of an attack and hopefully find him answers.

After a few brief niceties that were hallmark of the COS's conversations, Trowbridge jumped right to the purpose of his call. "I have made all the arrangements we discussed after the catastrophe in Iowa to activate the investigative team. I have informed Homeland Security, the FBI, ATF, and all concerned local police departments that they should assist you and minimize constraints. After careful thought of the needs of the task force, I've decided to add to your Mixed Martial Arts (MMA) group. I am also bringing on Nick Forrest from the Department of Homeland Security (DHS), and Tanya Anderson, the Chicago reporter we've hired as communications coordinator for DHS. Tanya can help us keep tabs on the media scuttlebutt.

I have set up the account that Christian will oversee, ordered special ID's for each of you, and contacted each of your employers about upcoming and unexpected travel. I also emailed you my comprehensive data file via SIPRNET (Secret Internet Protocol Router Network). I've also written a letter that you can show to the head of any department, as needed, and they should assist you and minimize delays. I am also providing you with secure satellite phones for all calls between us so that everything remains confidential. Any questions so far?"

"Well, Sir, I didn't expect to have someone from the media. Is that usual?" noting my heart leapt at the mention of her name, but I tamped it down quickly reminding myself that I must remain focused on the business at hand.

"Yes, in these days, it's better to have the media covered than scrambling to catch up. She is the face known everywhere from the attacks and people talk quite freely to her. It can be an advantage. Of course, she won't be traveling with you, but you will 'bump into her' from time to time. I am confident she will not compromise the investigation."

John's MMA group members were all current or former military and were highly trained to gather intelligence and to work with people who either wouldn't or were afraid to talk with anyone about their situations. Even with his group's expertise, he realized Trowbridge could be right. Having a woman who had lived through one of the attacks might encourage others to open up. It couldn't hurt. Personally, he didn't mind either.

I proceeded to review my investigative plan with the COS. "I have Owens and Hunt set to meet Nick Forrest in Las Vegas to go through the different locations and surrounding areas with him. They will investigate the suicide bombings at the different hotels, the Hoover Dam explosion, and the disaster on the Strip. Nick is a known contact to the authorities out there since he was involved in the immediate aftermath. He will ease the introductions. I have Griffin and Marks slated to go to Maryland and look into the hostage event at Chatham Academy and head over to Virginia to see Agent Troy McGinnis. Christian and I will travel to Iowa and then to Chicago."

"We will use family and historical site visits as part of our cover. We can also use some MMA events to cover areas we don't have relatives or any other obvious reason to be there. These things will keep us below the radar for the most part. The more seamless our entries, the less notice anyone will take of us."

"Good thinking," said Trowbridge. "You and I should talk at least weekly and more if necessary. I receive lots of information every day and I will help you in any way I can. By the way, I will call your team the President's Mighty Men, like David's Mighty Men from the Bible, and you can use that moniker to speak to anyone in my office. In the meantime, get your plans underway and I will facilitate your work situations as well. The sooner we get this underway, the better the President and I will both feel."

"Thanks, sir, this way we can move out quickly, how would the week after Thanksgiving work for starting our trips? That would give the team a week to clear up hot issues at work and spend the holiday with their families?"

"I can live with that," said Trowbridge, "but not any later."

Hanging up, I wished I felt free to send up a quick prayer, like all my friends did, for wisdom and understanding of what we would be seeing and learning. I then began the calls to my fellow MMA members to implement our plans. I laughed to myself at the COS's name for their unit. Was this another incident of God's interceding in my life? I would have to have a discussion with Christian on the matter. Perhaps I could talk with him on our travel to Iowa.

CHAPTER 4

Mustering the Team

Early in the morning, my phone rang and to my total surprise, it was COS Trowbridge. His voice urgent, he skipped the usual niceties that were his hallmark. "John, there has been an attack in Atlanta which is very suspicious and a real problem. We may be in for more trouble. I need you and Christian to go as quickly as possible. John, they killed the Sherriff with a sniper shot to the head! This is so hard to take in, call me as soon as you talk with the authorities there, ok?" Can you leave even though it is still the holiday weekend?" I can forward the necessary paperwork to the FBI offices at each of your individual destinations. "I will text you the name of the FBI coordinator in Atlanta. Just get started, son, just go!"

My immediate, "Yes, sir!" was sufficient for the COS and he ended the call.

I phoned my cohorts with the news of the new situation and Christian's and I immediate departure. All had the same short reaction ready to start our work. Christian and I moved into high gear, used to sudden movements as part of the military life, we each prepared to leave quickly.

During my preparations to leave, I took a quick look at the morning mail as I put the 'hold' note in the box. I noticed a letter from Evelyn's father and ripped it open. I stood in shock as I considered the contents of the letter. I barely knew how to take it. I would ask Christian about this, this and my other questions. The President chose me and my friends to investigate the horrendous attacks carried out by terrorists on four separate targets across the country. The terrorists who carried out these highly coordinated and skillful attacks were living in the country in clandestine terrorist camps. These people came into the nation and lived as neighbors and coworkers but harboring the underlying intent of attacking to support their cause against their adopted home. They had killed and maimed many people, destroyed businesses and part of the electrical grid on 10/10. Their actions created a sense of anger that had not been felt since the first attack on 9-11, 2001.

Because I had met the President during the future President's brief tour in the Army, I had written him during a visit with my late wife's parents. I was startled to hear the Muslim Call to Prayer in the middle of Iowa, the bread basket of the world and I had written the letter almost as an afterthought. However, the President's COS, Earnest Trowbridge contacted me shortly after receiving the note. It seemed that there was a lot of terrorist 'chatter' that no one had been able to decipher. my letter had given them a chilling answer. It was this contact with the President that had led to the formation of the team and the reason the COS dealt with me directly.

Christian and I began the journey to Atlanta about two hours after the COS's call, feeling dismay over such a problematic event on such a busy day. But I had questions for Christian that were at the forefront of my mind as we drove. After about half an hour of silent driving, I hesitantly said with a hushed voice, "Christian, do you remember our discussions about getting the folks in Iowa to talk freely with us?" At Christian's nod, I continued. "Well, when I put the note to hold my mail in my mailbox, the driver had already made his run for the day and I found a letter from Evelyn's father. He was asking that we come and talk with him and his neighbors about the events in their area. Does God arrange things for you when you need it? Is He really interested in the day-to-day things of our lives? I know this is a bit more of a world thing, these attacks, but is He involved in these kinds of things also? And what about my wife's death? Couldn't He have prevented that as well if He is so involved?" My voice rose in volume and speed as if I had to spit the questions out before I lost my nerve.

Since the accident, I struggled to believe that a 'loving God' would take my wife, who had loved God so fully. My friends also loved this same God but I still had questions about how this God, so great and powerful, let my wife die so young. The team had talked with me, answered questions, but not pushed me.

Christian's eyes widened and he stared at me for a second. "What's going on John? What are you talking about?"

I thrust the letter at him and just nodded. Christian read the letter with a bemused expression growing on his face. "Hmm, interesting. This could be a real open door. What do you think?"

I was so disconcerted that I missed the question all together. My response was an insistent, "does God do these types of things for you? I need to know!"

"Well, people tend to miss it and chalk it up to coincidence, but yes, He does. This could be a real opportunity for us since they have asked us and more open than usual to questions. Yes, God does open doors for His People, says so in the Bible. He will open and close doors to keep us on the right track."

"Then why didn't He close a door to keep Evelyn from being on that slick road that night?" was my anguished question.

"Ah, John, that is one of the mysteries that God hasn't revealed to us yet. But I can assure you that there is always a reason even if we don't understand it. I am sorry not to have a solid answer for you but we often go through things that we don't understand at the time but will later. But some, we will not understand this side of Heaven. This may be one of them."

"That's no comfort!" I spat back at him. "I've tried to figure out why, what did I do or not do that caused her death but nothing makes any sense. How can I find any peace, if I don't understand?"

"The comfort comes from knowing that God loves you, He loves Evelyn and knew that she loved Him. He didn't steal from you, it was her time in His scheme of things and He still has a plan for you that isn't complete. We all live with questions but when you are able to give it all to Him and trust His motives, no matter what, there is a peace that doesn't make sense but is very real. But right now, you need to consider why you feel you left something undone or did something that caused Evelyn's death. Why do you think this is your train of thought?"

"I don't know, it just feels so wrong to be here without her, you know?" the blood began to drain from my face, replaced by a pallor that concerned Christian as much as the flushing had.

"John, none of us have all the answers but my guess would be that you are suffering survivor's guilt. It's common among the military, really any survivors in any circumstances. Someone you have a bond with dies and you don't and you try to figure out why. There is only one why and it involves their time and purpose being fulfilled and yours not being. It is not much comfort to my way of thinking but I know it to be true. I have struggled with it myself. Why did some die and I remain. I don't honestly know, but I know that God has now revealed a new purpose for my life, all my training, all my understanding. It is pretty amazing when you think about it. I guess it has to do with perspective. And that goes for you also."

I stared at him for what seemed forever, and then uttered, "Oh. I will have to think about that. What about our mission and the letter?"

"Just as I said, John, God has opened a door for us and we need to walk right through it. It's actually a great opportunity. Call Trowbridge first thing in the morning and then we can plan our strategy. In fact, you said he called earlier and told you that everything is in place for our mission to begin. God's timing is always perfect. We will talk in the morning. Just think about this tonight and you'll eventually know the truth about God."

First thing the next morning, I notified Earnest of the letter and the extraordinary opportunity. This news caused a hardy, "Praise the Lord," out of Earnest who then quickly repeated that he was expediting our moves by saying he had already sent all the ID's and pertinent papers to the particular authorities by special courier. "After Atlanta, go on to Ames, Iowa, and then to Fort Dodge. When you arrive, contact the FBI agent still in the town trying to figure out more details of what had occurred in that area.

I acknowledged and allowed myself a grin of pure delight. I thought again that working with Earnest was going to be interesting. Having someone in charge of our endeavors who sought the Lord brought its own questions in my mind. This was a man of the world but was also a man of the Word, giving me more food for thought. The others would be thrilled. Things were sure moving fast now, and I had a lot to consider.

It took two days for the others to make the necessary preparations to begin their treks to the various other locations of the October 10th attacks. The team agreed to drive to their various locations, which would allow them flexibility to change course easily, without involving others in the planning. Although driving could be more hazardous because of the unpredictable fall weather, all of them were well-versed in travel problems and able to cope easily with the possibilities.

CHAPTER 5

On the Move

Glad for the six AM start in Atlanta, we finally rolled into Fort Dodge, Iowa about eight in the evening. They quickly checked into the Best Western Starlight Village Inn, relishing the pleasant 2 bed suite that offered a place to work plus ample sitting and relaxing space. We hustled down to the Buford Steak House restaurant on the premises for a bite to eat.

I called my in-laws to let them know I was in town and arranged to meet for breakfast the next morning. We hurried through preparations for sleep and lay down in an exhausted state.

Meanwhile, the same early start found Dan Griffin and Bill Marks close to Silver Springs, Maryland. Their day had been a meandering journey though mountainous areas of Alabama, Tennessee, and Virginia, a beautiful but tiring ride. At six in the evening, it was already dark and they sought the closest hotel complex for their stay. The Hampton Inn on Colesville Road gave them the comfort and flexibility they desired. It was short work to check in and take on the gym for some restorative workouts after a long drive. After quick showers, they headed out to the Fijita Coast restaurant for a meal to top of a day of fast food stops on their almost 12-hour, 718-mile trip. Excited and a bit restless, they none the less wisely retired to their room for the night.

Jeremy Hunt and Marcus Owens began their trek with Jeremy driving and Marcus on his cell phone, calling his relatives in Henderson, Nevada to let them know of his impending arrival with a friend. His folks were used to the Green Beret officer's sudden visits, snatched from his military schedule and were delighted to hear of his visit.

About midnight two days later, they rolled into Las Vegas to the bright lights and noise of a city that is full of revelry 24/7, 365 days a year. Following the directions forwarded to them by Forrest, they located the quiet road behind all the glitz and the hotel that offered a serene place to sleep, talk together without garnering attention, and follow-up on any leads that Forrest would have by now. It was central without the hustle and bustle of Las Vegas Boulevard. A quick snack, a shower each and the room settled into the silence of weary sleepers.

Each of the three sets of investigators was enjoying the idea of having a puzzle to figure out, stories to learn, and bad guys to catch. None had any thought that this trip might be dangerous. They were enjoying the adventure and looking forward to finally doing something positive. But now, there had been another attack and it no longer seemed an adventure but a deadly pursuit of terrible people set on destroying the peace of their nation.

The next morning, each team in their respective cities, linked up with the local police, DHS and FBI sources. Earnest Trowbridge had fulfilled his promises to the fullest extent so there was little to no delay in making the needed contacts and being "read in" on the local personnel's information. Seeing those who had dealt with the events in progress gave an up-close and personal feeling to their activities. It deepened the idea that this was no longer just an adventure but a serious endeavor to find the culprits.

Earnest Trowbridge stood inside his office pondering the ways of God and man. In the last months, he felt as if he had seen the worst of man and the best of God working through other men and women. The attacks of October had thrown the country into a state of panic greater than even the nine-eleven attacks in 2001. The terrorist had hit targets across the nation in a sequence that left no doubt as to the level of planning and coordination used by these terrorists. He couldn't say they were 'mad' because their ability to carry out such detailed attacks could not be done by mad men. Devious, malicious, evil, thoroughly inhuman but certainly not crazy, not in the sense most people considered crazy.

His thoughts turned to the team he was waiting to meet with, seven men and one woman. Some had experienced the attack days up close and personal or were part of his strategic inner group to investigate and hopefully run the perpetrators to ground. He had sent the team of six from Redstone Arsenal in Alabama out to each of the sites of the attacks to determine background information. The six were former Special Forces members or military intelligence officers, active duty or retired from the different services. Each worked at Redstone Arsenal which is also famous for the NASA's research in the space and rocket fields. Huntsville, Alabama was the final home of Werner Von Braun, the leader of the Space program for the US and also home of the Space Camp program.

Earnest never stopped being amazed at the level of educational prowess in the area. Also, about an hour south of Huntsville was Birmingham, Alabama, where leaders in medicine helped develop the medical expertise for NASA to put a man on the moon. People tended to laugh at the cartoon of Alabama being backward but it was far from the actual truth and he was happy to work with these people, who had great knowledge and character.

He considered the fact that God had brought John Banks to his attention when John wrote a letter to the President alerting authorities of the presence of terrorist camps in the country. John had roomed with President David Brooks for a short time as the future President did a stint in the military. The other team members were John's associates; who Earnest had informally made leader of the group in Alabama because of his relationship with the President. Christian Blade, a retired Navy Seal and instructor at the military EOD School, (Explosive Ordinance Disposal School,) served as his teammate. Marcus Owen, a retired Green Beret Officer, Dan Griffin, former Army Intel officer, Jeremy Hunt, retired Air Force Intel Officer, and Bill Marks, retired Navy Intel Officer, rounded out the original team. All were civilian employees of the Army, each using the skills learned on active duty to do the work involved around the military's acquisition research programs.

The seventh man was Homeland Security Agent, Nick Forrest, lead DHS agent in Las Vegas last October. His one lady, Tanya Anderson, was the reporter who was taping a segment for TV at the Chicago Mercantile Exchange as the attack took place. Her report seen nationally in her bloody, dusty clothes made her the symbolic icon of the day. Each of the eight had a unique perspective on the events and he looked forward to hearing in person what they had determined from their visits to each of the sites.

This was their first face to face meeting since the 10 October attacks and the early November disastrous failure in Iowa where they lost some good men from the FBI and ATF. He felt as cold inside as the brisk December day. There had been an extremely short period of quiet in November until the Thanksgiving holiday truck bombing in Atlanta on Black Friday. Earnest had sent John and Christian to Atlanta after the attack there and afterwards they had traveled to Iowa and then to Chicago.

His team of investigators visited each of the now six attack sites and interviewed the people in those areas. The only one not visiting the sites was Tanya since he had moved her to the Department of Homeland Security Communications Office. He also arranged for Nick Forrest's transfer to Huntsville effective immediately after he facilitated the Las Vegas and Hoover Dam interviews for Owens and Hunt. The move would allow him to work closely with the team as he was coming in as the DHS consultant. The existence of the team was secret and few people knew anything about it. While he had arranged for their involvement in the investigation, no one outside his office knew they worked for him.

Earnest walked into the conference where the team was waiting and after a few brief pleasantries, asked Christian to open their meeting with a short prayer. He did so thanking God for his help and guidance and also asking for wisdom and discernment for their investigations. Earnest then nodded to John and said, "Why don't you guys start with Atlanta, since it was the latest attack.

CHAPTER 6

The Gathering of Minds, December 12th

I started, "Christian and I left Atlanta after the last of the victims were transported to the local hospitals and went to Ames, Iowa. We didn't get anything concrete from our short time in Atlanta, but we made some good contacts while there especially with the Chief of Police.

Two other team members, Dan Griffin and Bill Marks, checked out things in Maryland and Virginia. The last two members, Marcus Owens and Jeremy Hunt went to Las Vegas and talked with some of the same people Forrest interviewed but from the perspective of the national security so that we could move forward in finding the fiends who did this to our country."

I then turned the briefing over to Dan and Bill. "Dan why don't you start."

Dan started by saying, "Maryland was probably the hardest to investigate since it involved the treatment of children during a hostage situation. The worse thing for each of us was listening to the tape of the terrorist forcing a second-grade boy to answer the phone after the siege was underway and then selecting him as one of the student hostages afterwards. The boy is home with his parents receiving care from a PTSD specialist. He still has nightmares and fears which keep him home. The parents are home schooling him as part of this therapy.

I could see the anger and sorrow crossing the faces of the team as they listened to the account.

Bill picked up the narration by stating, "The men captured during the escape attempt continued to refuse to say anything at all. One of those captured attempted suicide but was foiled when an alert prison guard found him hanging from his bed frame. The others just maintain a surly manner and say nothing. Their leader slipped away in the confusion of the capture in the mountains of Virginia.

The team enjoyed a brief moment of comic relief when Dan and Bill recounted their interview with Farmer Rivers and met the famous bull, Big Ben.

Bill continued, "Unfortunately there has not been any reported sightings of the terrorist leader called into our hotline but since we only had the school personnel's description of the man, no one was particularly surprised, disappointed yes, surprised, no.

Glancing at his watch, Trowbridge said, "Why don't we take a short break to use the restrooms and refill coffee." So, the group broke up, everyone noticing the Tanya and I made great efforts to stay away from each other.

I began my report about Ames by reaching into my folder and bringing out a small brochure. "We found in Ames, the Real Estate Broker whose office had handled all the sales for the properties used by the terrorists. She was shocked to learn this and checked her records. All the sales were handled by one agent who had disappeared within days of the attacks."

"Returning to her office the day after that agent disappeared, she found even his picture was missing from the wall. She filed a missing persons report on him but had never heard anything back. She found one brochure in her file cabinet with his picture when she had filed the report and willingly turned it over to us. The file cabinet was the only one in the office she kept locked. This is the only picture of the man. All the other pictures of him were taken, including the larger one on the wall.

This revelation that we had a picture of one of the men electrified the team. The room erupted in comments and Earnest quickly clapped his hands to quieten them, saying, "Let's get back to the business at hand."

Continuing on with my report, I explained, "We traveled north to Fort Dodge and talked with the local residents which was made easier by my late wife's father. We heard the local Iowans express anger and fear because they had accepted these people into their community. Although the newcomers had kept to themselves and were quiet, the locals were devastated to learn that they appeared to have been a part of the October attacks. They were personally affronted by the massacre of FBI and ATF agents in early November during the failed raid on the compound. A miserable failure that somehow seemed their fault! Frightened to be so unaware of the number of terrorists hiding in their small community, their anger was intense, their fear palatable.

During the investigation after the massacre, the investigators found a number of tunnels and cave dwellings that hid the exact number of men on the grounds. The team also found clear signs of training sites, now abandoned. This is another group that seems to have just walked off the face of the earth.

Following a brief investigation after she filed the report, the police found no hint or trace of the missing 'realtor's existence. He left no signs of his existence at the office or his apartment, no fingerprints, no DNA, nothing."

Christian then talked about the attack in Chicago. "The terrorists hit both the FBI office and the Chicago Mercantile Exchange. The FBI office suffered minimal damage because an alert agent saw the truck barreling across the open courtyard in front of the building. Taking quick action, the agent shot the driver causing the truck to veer to the left, crashing into a fountain injuring five civilians mostly from debris from the impact of the truck.

The civilian injuries were of the minor kind because everyone ran from the erratic vehicle before it slammed into the fountain. Thankfully no one at the FBI office was injured and after an extensive search by the agents, the truck was found to have had ties to a Farris Construction Company."

Christian continued, "It was a different story at the Chicago Mercantile Exchange building. The terrorists succeeded in killing five members of the Board of Directors in the explosion, severely wounding two others. The current death toll stands at ten for now. There were seven staff members in the building to assist the Directors, all but one of whom died in the blasts. Some of the wounded are still in critical condition due to severe burns and there could be more deaths. Our current total is fifteen dead which includes two firemen. Other than film of the three shadowy men fleeing from the building just before the explosions, the locals don't have any specifics about this attack. Tanya's cameraman captured the three figures while filming a segment about the Board meeting before he was injured by the blast. They both were knocked down by the explosion and it is considered a miracle they are still alive. We are all aware that Tanya suffered a concussion and cuts from debris but rose to the occasion to tell what happened live in front of the burning building, still wearing her dirty and tattered clothing." Christian gave a nod in her direction while talking about her.

I took a peek at Tanya, noticing her blush as her part was discussed; it grew deeper over the 'rising to the occasion remark. Everyone paying attention noticed the deepening blush. They all considered her their personal heroine of that day.

The group sat in silence as they digested the information. Having someone so directly involved with one of the events working with them made the whole thing personal for each of them.

After a minute, Earnest turned to Nick Forrest and waved his hand to indicate it was time for his report.

Nick Forrest began by speaking of the mess in Las Vegas and Boulder Dam. "Damage is estimated in the millions and maybe more because of the nature of the Casinos. There was a serious loss of vital services after a number of ambulances were destroyed. Las Vegas also is seeing a loss of income to the city, a major problem. The economic base for Las Vegas is in the Casinos and the visitors they bring to the city. Visits to the area have been way down because of the fear generated by such destruction coming out of the blue. While understandable, it is still a major blow to the economy of the area. There is hope that this can be overcome soon.

The Electrical Farm is a total loss. It will take a great deal of time and money to get that back into service. If the President hadn't immediately commanded the entire national electrical network to begin allocating power to the areas hit the hardest, the south west from Arizona to the coast of California would be worse than the current struggle to reduce brownouts that they are struggling under now.

Investigators found a badly charred body in the electrical farm control site that burned when the terrorist slammed trucks into the transformer towers. The police tentatively identified the body as the young man I questioned at the Las Vegas Airport based on body size and the fact that he has disappeared, but without fingerprints or dental records, nothing is sure.

The key lead we gathered is the report from several Boulder Dam employees of seeing three trucks with a large black horse imprinted on the side. The writing on the side alongside the horse was some construction company but after checking no one found orders for any construction for that area. There is work around the bridge over the gorge which is a good distance from the actual dam, plus the company working that site states categorically that they didn't have any trucks in the area around the Dam or electric farm. Forensic reconstruction of one of the trucks to hit the electric farm showed a faint outline of a horse. As best we can determine, these trucks are possibly tied to a Farris Construction Company and we forwarded this information to the FBI lead for this investigation."

Following an energetic discussion, Trowbridge spoke what everyone was thinking. "Besides the whole Academy thing in Maryland, this Farris Construction Company seems to be the one consistent clue in this whole scenario of attacks. Let's begin with a thorough investigation into this company."

Everyone agreed and following a short prayer, the meeting ended.

CHAPTER 7

Is that Romance in the Air?

With everyone tired but keyed up after the meeting, each adjourned to their separate hotel room except Tanya who had a small apartment near the Pentagon area. She now lived in Washington and was worn out from the intensity of their meeting as well as trying to ignore John. This was hard on two accounts; he was the primary leader of the group after the COS and so was not easy to ignore. Even more tiring was that she still struggled with her attraction to him since she had first laid eyes on him. It was frustrating that they had never spoken more than fifty words to each other and then only about their jobs. But she still dreamed of him at night and the attraction felt stronger each time she saw him. He lived in Alabama and she in D.C. and she didn't see things going any further. She remained unaware of any feelings on his part because his emotions remained quite stoic.

I lay down on my bed in the room I shared with Christian and closed my eyes. But it wasn't Christian or even their investigation that were front and center of my thoughts; it was Tanya, her burnished auburn hair and those azure eyes haunt my dreams. I wondered if there would ever be a time one of them wasn't running here or there to do something pertaining to the crisis that had brought us together. What would happen when all this was over? Would I ever even see her again? These were the questions that kept me slightly off balance emotionally.

I wondered for a second what Christian would think of my thoughts? And decided I didn't want to venture into that territory with my friend, no man, not for a second! But I was interested in knowing more about the beautiful young woman who haunted my nights and occupied a lot of my thoughts when I was awake. I had seen her background check and knew that she was from Birmingham, Alabama. A nice fit for me in Huntsville, if? If What? Just what was I thinking? I shook my head to dispel these crazy thoughts; sure, it wouldn't do any good.

The next morning all us staying at the hotel met for breakfast and the talk centered on Nick's move to Huntsville. He was in the process of moving and was asking a lot of questions about the town, where to live, what the town was like, etc.

Christian, along with the others, tried to answer him as much as possible, finally agreeing that it was really unlike any other place they had lived. It was a military town for sure, but also home of the research side of Space exploration making it home to a large number of PHDs that gave it a very different flavor from most military towns. We suggested that he look around when he arrived and we would help him to find a place. I told him to begin at the complex where my apartment was located, close to the base but nice and quiet. Nick just nodded and we headed to the airport to arrive home in about six hours. I shared with Nick the standing joke in Alabama that even to get to heaven you would probably have a stop in Atlanta since all trips usually seem to take that route and everyone laughed.

Satisfied that their involvement in the investigation of the 10-10 attacks were probably over despite the professional interest in what the FBI came up with about the truck bomb in Atlanta, the team settled back into our jobs and family routines. So until or when we found any of the culprit leaders, we thought our roles were done.

CHAPTER 8

December 14th, Enemy Gambit

Fletcher Cordell had inserted two special students, Jerry Walsh, a student from Great Britain, and Harold Harris, a native of Slovenia, and now they were holed up in their tiny apartment located on the tree lined street across from Massachusetts Avenue in the historic theater district of Boston. The Symphony Hall which housed the Boston Pops Orchestra and the Boston Opera House where the famed Nutcracker Ballet performances were performed and were in full swing for the holiday season. The apartments were mainly occupied by students of the many surrounding colleges and universities and those students were the mainstay of temporary staff for these iconic music programs offering world class performances.

Jerry's job was on the maintenance staff of the Symphony Hall, Harold, had the same type of job at the Opera House. They were transfer students here to study engineering and were quiet members of the local Mosque. Each had taken an Arabic name when they had converted to Islam but they used them only at the Mosque. It was a connection unknown to their fellow students or their employers. No one paid much attention to either as they worked hard, were quiet, and kept to themselves

Fletcher Cordell listened by phone as the Assistant Imam brought him up on the current status of their plan.

"I told them about the first part of the assignment you sent them here to perform. I showed them the small lab we set up for them and they are satisfied with the set up. The extinguishers were all in place. It looks similar to a small kitchen set up to serve small groups. They have all the equipment needed in the cabinets, to include gloves to protect them as they work. Everything is in order for the task at hand and I will inform you when they are complete. They know their jobs and the danger inherent to it.

On December 20th, Jerry and Harold entered the small lab and began the final preparations for the upcoming mission. After completing the very careful transfer of the contents of the canisters to the extinguishers, they too left and disappeared into the night. Later, no one ever acknowledged their existence or presence in the Mosque.

According to Cordell's very specific instructions, the men arrived for work early, shivering in the cold with an extra undertone of excitement. This is preparation for the day they were born for. Each had gone to the Mosque for a special blessing by the Imam for their work. They received their final instructions and a blessing from Cordell.

Setting about their usual tasks, first of which was inspecting each of the fire extinguishers located in the buildings. It was vital to the plan that everything appeared normal. The night before, December 23rd, as everyone was leaving for the night after the evening performance, the two men sneaked back in through the guest entrances as the audience left was easy since both Jerry and Harold wore the uniform of a staff member. Ignored by the ushers as they assisted people out into the cold, clear night, Jerry went into the restroom on the second floor of the Symphony

Hall and hid in one of the stalls. Harold had done exactly the same at the Concert Hall. They were in place for the most important part of the mission set up.

After waiting an hour after the noise died down, Jerry and Harold each left his hiding place and moved confidently through the buildings. Their fellow conspirators were waiting in the dark at the employee entrance with their deadly cargo. Both turned off the alarms, and opened the doors, allowing everyone quietly inside. The men who had brought the special fire extinguishers carried them carefully to the chosen places in the highest areas of the buildings. Sarin gas, being heavier than air, would sink down to the audience in deadly silence. The actual work was not hard, only the careful changing out of their extinguishers for the regular ones was time consuming. The night watchman slowed the progress as they had to work around his rounds. They had trained for this mission intensively in the 'lab' and the work went smoothly. When the work was complete, each man moved silently to the exit carrying the regular extinguishers and Jerry and Harold, being last out, reset the door alarms and slid out into the night. Their excitement from the smooth start of the mission numbed them to the cold during their walk home. They took extra measures to avoid being seen during this late-night stroll. They could not take the chance of a late-night transit worker or anyone remembering them being in the area on this night. In the end, it would not matter but they didn't want to create any suspicions this close to the attack.

CHAPTER 9

Revenge of the Rat King

The afternoon performance time arrived and the crowd began entering the building. The Opera House was crowded but everyone was respectful. Because of their Holiday spirit, the excited children danced in place as they moved slowly into the theater. Many considered this the foundation of the excitement of Christmas, seeing the annual performance of the Nutcracker at the famed house. It was a family tradition for many of those in attendance.

The ballet started like any other performance, but at the end of Act I reached its climax with the slaying of the Mouse King. The music soared increasing the level of the drama and no one noticed the quiet hissing over the celebration of the Mouse King's death.

The roar of the celebration turned into a roar of terror filled cries and panic as those in the balcony noticed bleeding from their noses and mouths. Soon even those in the lower levels experienced the bleeding and severe nausea followed by vomiting. The music died in a cacophony as the orchestra began to feel the effects of 'something'. On the main floor, panic ensued as first one or two, and then a crowd stumbled to their feet, thinking only to get out of the building. They didn't make it. Some in the crowd collapsed to the floor creating an obstacle course for the other attendees.

Someone in the back managed to dial 911, reporting the situation before falling to the floor. Slowly the sound dropped and the great hall fell to a morbid silence with the only sound the labored breathing or retching of people. Death strolled in to silence those still struggling.

Within a quarter of an hour, emergency people arrived with protective gear to work the incident. The words on the 911 tape alerted them to the possibility of a gas leak or maybe worse. With similar incidents happening in such close proximity, the Emergency Management Team for the city, were speculating that this was not a normal gas leak.

The sight inside turned the first responders' stomachs as they took in the sight of all these people in their holiday finery covered in vomit, blood, and other bodily fluids, some barely breathing or not moving, still laying where they fell on the floor. The people in the upper balconies seemed to have been hit worse than those in the lower areas; the CSI teams began their investigation by taking blood and fluid samples plus DNA samples. This was the fastest way to determine the cause of such devastation and eventually make a positive identification of those lost in the attack. At the famed Boston Pops, similar protocols were underway, and although they were pretty sure the food on the main floor was not the issue, they took samples just in case. Similar to the Opera House the people in the balcony areas were affected the most.

The medical teams at both theaters began helping those who seemed the most responsive and checking those who were unresponsive. The majority of the unresponsive were already dead, but a small few were alive, but in a comatose state. The heartbreaking fact was that most of the dead were children.

CHAPTER 10

If it Bleeds It Leads

BREAKING NEWS FROM WHNT, CHANNEL 19, and on WVNN, 92.5 FM, Huntsville, Alabama

"We interrupt your programming to bring you breaking news from Boston; Police are reporting two attacks in the famous Boston Theater district during an afternoon matinee showing of the Nutcracker and a Christmas performance by the world-famous Boston Pops Orchestra. We are receiving these reports about the attacks from our CBS affiliate in Boston. We go there now for the latest.

The news station shifted to the CBS affiliate in Boston;"This is Amy Stroud from CBS in Boston, although everything is still up in the air, we are getting indications that this is a possible gas leak or gas attack. It appears that first responders are wearing protective gear reminiscent of the Sarin gas attacks in Tokyo. I should get more information at the scheduled press brief in ½ an hour."

The TV shifted back to the local station and the reporter stated: "There is little information available at this time but we will continue to monitor the situation and keep you informed of any breaking news. Stay tuned for more information."

Oval Office, Washington D.C

Earnest Trowbridge, the President's COS, walked into the Oval Office with his usual decorum but admitted that his heart was beating at a high rate. The President had seldom summoned him unexpectedly to the Oval Office, the only other time being on October 10th, a day he would never forget. As he entered, the President, David Brooks, was running his hands through his hair in an anguished manner and turned as the door opened.

Earnest heard anger and fear in the President's voice as he spoke, turning back to stare out the window of the Oval Office.

"Earnest, what have we done to deserve this? They've hit us again, at Christmas, in Boston; they have struck at both the Boston Pops Christmas concert and the performance of the Nutcracker! So many people are hurt; they think it might be Sarin gas. Why do they continue to do this?" As he vented to his surrogate father, he began to slow down and then raised his hand to stop Earnest's reply. "O, sure, I know they hate us for merely existing and want to show us their power. But it is so senseless to especially hurt children in this way. These guys are real monsters. We saw it in Iraq and Syria with ISIS but to assault the two shows that mean Christmas to so many is below the belt! Earnest, we talked about going to the performances over the holiday week! What do we do? Bomb everywhere and let the chips fall where they may?"

Earnest stood quietly as he prayed for guidance. "The country has handled so much in the last months but this, this will send everyone into total panic...or total angry fight mode. Consider the group I talked with earlier this month, I know they will react with anger but I trust that those prepared for combat would think through what they should do and not run off halfcocked."

The President threw up his hands, saying, "I was certainly disappointed in what they were able to find out in their trips across the country to check out the four attack sites of 10/10 and I know you were also. In a nutshell, the enemy has completely disappeared. They all assured me that this was normal for terrorist groups. My one hope is the information John and, is it Christian, turned up in Ames, Iowa? They got not only the name but a small picture of one of the culprits. Can we hope that we can build on that even though the man did disappear just a week after the October attacks? There has been no information on the man; he was in no data bases, not even the foreign ones!"

"I think the people will take this attack even harder because it involves children, people always get more riled up when children are hurt or involved. Many of the dead are children! Where is God in this?! This attack was straight out of hells handbook. They attacked during the Christmas Eve matinees, deliberately, to make sure they got the children. I have got to address this and although there will be plenty of anger and recriminations to go around, I need to find a way to focus that anger and not start chaos during the holidays."

Earnest gently asked, "What has the intelligence community reported, what exactly do we know? Have there been any specific reports as to the injuries or deaths besides the fact of the children? David, look at me, we will work this out but we need to know facts, not just what is coming over the T.V., we need to get the FBI and Homeland Security involved. I would also like to dispatch some of the guys from Redstone to get a look at the scene while it is fresh."

David shook his head. "No, I have not heard anything except that a lot of people are affected and in need of care. If it was Sarin, the affects can last a long time; Japan still has people suffering nineteen or more years after the subway attack." He paused to take a deep breath.

"In the aftermath of 10/10, I looked up some of this stuff. This is one of the nastiest gases, you can't smell, see, or hear it. You just get ill and die. And it works fast, one to ten minutes. If we can't run these scoundrels to earth, what else will happen?"

Earnest murmured as word of encouragement, "hold on and give me a minute," he patted David on the shoulder in support. He then left and hurried back to his office, forming plans as he went. It was imperative that they touch bases with their team and he was on the way to do just that. Three quick phone calls and it was done.

CHAPTER 11

Life Interrupted!

I was on the internet skyping with Tanya Anderson when her phone rang. She said, "I need to take this, it's from Ernest, please wait. After only a moment, she gasped and I quickly asked her, "What's wrong, Tanya?"

Tanya held up one finger, asking for a moment, as she talked on her phone for another minute. I heard her say, "Yes, Sir, I'll be right over." She then turned to me and said, "John, there have been attacks at both the Boston Pops Christmas concert and the performance this afternoon of the Nutcracker! Earnest wants to talk via VTC (Video Tele Conferencing). Since I was already talking with you, he said to tell you and the team to go to the secure conference room at AMC headquarters. He has already spoken with the Commander and it is all set. I am to meet him at the White House conference room in about half an hour so we will all be available to consider what we want to do. I'll see you then."

I murmured, "OK" and we both hung up. I immediately called Christian Blade, and we following our teams standard operating procedures (SOP) would call the other four, two each. I would call Nick Forrest who was in the middle of settling into his new apartment on Rideout Road.

They had about twenty-five minutes to call and get to AMC headquarters. I gave a thanks to 'someone' that everyone was in town this Christmas Eve.

Earnest returned to the Oval Office to find David still in a state of frustration.

David spoke as if Earnest had never left the room. "It sounds like they have a stronger strain than what was used in Japan. That is not good, no, really not good. People will suffer a long time if they live. Children are being affected more just because they are small and the gas is stronger. I'm trying really hard not to say what I am thinking out loud, Earnest, I think some part of your faith is rubbing off. But, and it's a big but, why would your God allow this to happen as we celebrate His Son's birth? And so many children? Why?" David turned to stare out the window as Earnest picked up the phone and notified the Secret Service that they were moving to the secure Conference Room.

Earnest again quickly asked for wisdom under his breath. "David, we live in an evil world with evil on every corner. God doesn't 'allow' this stuff; it is unfortunately part of living in the midst of evil. And His Word says that it will be really bad toward the end. This is certainly bad enough for me wherever we are in His time table. Let's see what our team says about this. They are on their way to a secure conference room at Redstone Arsenal; Tanya is on her way here and we will meet in the secure conference room. Fortunately, she was skyping with John when I called her. The men should be in place in 10 or so minutes. I arranged all this after you informed me and, in any case, we will need to consider their input. It will be good to hear their perspective on this. We need some wisdom and reality."

CHAPTER 12

Death Meets a VTC

At 5:36 pm in Huntsville, we were all set in the Headquarters Army Materiel Command Secure conference room and the team was present for the VTC with Earnest and the President. The call came through and they could see the two men with Tanya in the White House secure room. It was 6:36 pm there.

David nodded to his COS.

Trowbridge spoke quietly, "Hello to each of you and thank you for joining us so quickly. There have been two attacks confirmed, one at the Concert Hall and the other at the Opera House in Boston. There are many casualties, many children, and the worst is that the attackers are currently suspected to have used Sarin gas at both shows. We don't know at this time how the gas was released or even how it was delivered to the two buildings. The local authorities are just now starting to move the dead to TD Gardens Arena. They are transporting the ill to area hospitals as quickly as possible. The Christmas holiday shoppers and theater goers are hampering the evacuation because they are crowding the areas and have become gawkers. The local police are cordoning off the area and have asked for federal assistance. We need to determine how we get involved in this situation."

The men, visibly affected, had maintained their military stoicism. Tanya, on the other hand, whom everyone in Huntsville could see behind Earnest, let her silent tears run down her face. They all understood that her emotions were still heightened since the earlier attacks. She swiped at her tears a few times with her hand and Earnest seeing her situation, handed her his handkerchief. Silence swayed over them all, like a fog on an early fall morning.

The President broke the spell, suddenly pushing forward, "I want all of you in Boston. I want to **know** that I am receiving the best possible intelligence and analysis of the situation. I know the locals and other Federal agencies are competent but they are too close to the situation, as well as shorthanded. Right now, I want my handpicked team there to direct the efforts and give me the truth, not politically motivated information; what they think I want to hear. Can you all leave for Boston this afternoon? The COS can arrange the transportation from here if you are available. I know it's Christmas Eve but the whole country is already up in arms or emotionally distraught. I need some level heads there and that is this team. Go get me the underlying secrets! Find these terrorist for me!"

Earnest lightly tapped him on the shoulder and David nodded and turned away.

Earnest turned to them, "Guys, this is important, is there anything in the way of your leaving right away? I can have a transport ready for you in an hour, but I need to begin the process as soon as I can. Are you in?"

We all said, "Yes sir."

"Ok, I'll get on it at my end. You notify your families and try to be ready within the hour. I'll call if anything changes. Thank you for your wiliness to do this. I know it's a blow to family Christmas plans but I, and the President, need you on this."

The screen went dark.

The men turned to leave when Dan spoke, "I think we need to pray before we get in the rush of preparations." All the men agreed and turned to hold hands, even me. Christian prayed, "Lord, this is a terrible problem and we ask for your wisdom and insight in dealing with such a situation. We need you to lead us in the investigation and help us to learn the five W's of what happened. Please be with all the families that are and will be touched by this incident, thank you in Jesus' Name. Amen."

Everyone began to leave quickly to gather their things and say a quick goodbye to family and for the two single men to make arrangements for their apartments. As they exited the Command Building, Nick gave a quick laugh, "Well, I wasn't looking forward to Christmas alone but this is not how I thought it would go,"

I answered, "No, none of us wanted something like this, but you would not have been alone, the families would have called on us with presents and food tomorrow, they always have, and I for one am sorry to miss that."

CHAPTER 13

Counter Moves

As the team climbed into the plane, I watched each enter; glad to have such people on the team. Although I was loosely responsible for the team, I acknowledged each one's expertise. They were all professionals and I'd staked my life more than once on the competence and sincerity of my fellow team mates.

Christian, Marcus, Jeremy, Dan, Nick, and Bill, joined me on the chartered plane and it took off immediately. No one spoke as they settled in for the ride. Each had contacted family members about this new assignment and spent a short time regretting lost holidays. They each had experienced many lost holidays in their lives as military men. Their thoughts soon began to consider the possibilities of this new attack and how they would handle their part of the investigation. They had hoped that the October attacks would the last, especially in light of the way the attacks sequenced on October tenth but with terrorist attacks, nothing was sure.

Each team member was mulling over in their minds the past events of the last few months as they flew northward. The truck blast under an overpass in Atlanta had killed and maimed a large number of people. It had tied up traffic for months coming on Black Friday in November. It was the busiest shopping day of the year and the roads were crowded with people from many outlining areas. It was also happened close to the State Capitol building and the main Police Station in the city. The additional horror of the Atlanta Sherriff shot on live TV by a sniper caused a panic to start seeping through the city.

Ernest Trowbridge was getting an update brief on the current attacks from the Department of Homeland Security and the FBI on their progress on the 10/10 attacks. They were still digging through tons of paperwork trying to figure out the source of the truck used in the Atlanta attack as well as the vehicles used in the 10/10 attacks. The titles were so muddled; it was like trying to pull one string out of a ball of twine.

They had discovered a possible pattern and investigative teams were working constantly on the web of shadow corporations. The only thing they knew for certain was that these smaller companies were bought several months before the incidents and sold just before or right after an incident.

And now, with these two consecutive attacks in Boston at the height of the Christmas Season, the terrorist upped their game with the suspected use of Sarin gas. The terrorist choices were macabre as each attack was against areas so typical of American life. What brought it all together in the minds of the intelligence community was the combination of schools, financial entities, Las Vegas, and Christmas, if you added apple pie and a coke you had America essentially nailed down.

Back on the plane, the team's thoughts were interrupted by a phone call from the COS. Ernest updated us on the latest briefing and told us he was going to bring a few others in on the status of the team. Ernest said; "We will need to let a few more people know what your status is for your mission in Boston. No one on the team cared for the idea but knew that to be effective, some authorities would have to know their status. Our concern was that this kind of information too often slipped out. This would make it harder for the team to move around freely and ask questions, but these were hard times and we knew they just might get harder.

After the phone call, I doled out assignments, "I will interview the first officers on the scene. Dan and Bill, you cover the Boston Pops Concert Hall, Christian, Marcus and Jeremy, you can cover the Ballet Theater, Tanya and Nick are at the nearest Police Station reviewing what little they had on hand of the recordings from both locations. She will provide a statement for the President's office once it is written and Okayed by the COS.

CHAPTER 14

Investigating Death's Handiwork

I sought out Jason Carson, the site commander responding to the Boston Pops performance and felt the anger, hurt, and fear permeating the entire police force in the area. Carson was to the point. "I looked at the scene and recalled the information I studied of the Tokyo subway Sarin attack back in 1995. It killed twelve and injured more than six thousand in the subway. I studied it carefully after 10/10. My first thought was to figure out how such a gas, if this is a gas, was released into the theater. As I thought this through, my phone beeped. I was frozen in shock as the dispatcher told me that a call had also come in from the Opera House where the afternoon performance of the Nutcracker was interrupted by similar complaints, difficulty in breathing, bloody noses, vomiting, and loss of consciousness. My stomach sunk and I'm ashamed to admit it but I threw up in reaction. I just made it to the trash can. I immediately called the Fire Chief to inform him of the incidents, and my suspicions. I then called all levels of law enforcement including DHS, telling them that I strongly suspected terrorist attacks in Boston once again.

Man, I have never been this mad before but you probably understand the feelings."

I nodded, with a growing need to find answers and fast. I touched my ear piece to make a link up with the team, briefing them on my findings. Christian responded immediately but the background noise from the Theater made communication difficult. Christian did say "The strongest working theory is that the perps used Sarin gas, because of the victims' symptoms and initial blood work done on site are showing its presence. The EMTs transported those still alive to local hospitals and the other first responders are trying to identify the dead. Progress is slow because there a lot of children without IDs and few people present who might know them well enough to positively identify these bodies. The current plan is to move them to the T.D. Gardens Arena, home of the Boston Celtics and Bruins, the Boston Emergency Management Team plan to use this or other large under roof arenas in the case of large-scale incidents like this one. T.D. Gardens is closest to the two sites in question. The Red Cross and other emergency service organizations are in the process of trying to find family members who can give a positive identification."

I acknowledged him and turned to Carson. "What is the possibility that this was an inside job? I really don't see how it could have been done without help from the inside. We still do not know how the gas was introduced and we will have to examine every piece of equipment in the two buildings."

Carson stood silent as he considered my question. "I guess it is possible but it seems horrible to consider it. Most of the employees have been with the theaters for a good while but a lot of lower positions are filled with students from the universities around Boston. I will start with that roster. This is so disgusting, the pressure cooker bombs at the Marathon were bad but this takes the cake for worst ever attack on this city. I can start the coordination for our police labs to provide you and your team all of our findings, where should we focus our efforts?"

I nodded and said, "Start in the most logical place where a gas could be hidden, my mind goes to something that would create an aerosol effect. Do they have items in the bathrooms for smells, or... or, fire extinguishers? Those would be in the open and ignored by everyone. Let's start there!"

Carson called over the police channels to his lead investigator and said, "Gather all the fire extinguishers and any aerosol cans in the restrooms especially in the upper floors. I want them analyzed immediately by our lab techs. Have the men handle them carefully! We don't need any further injuries."

I could hear the affirmative answer and acknowledged my surprise at the quickness of my idea on this matter. I knew that my team and the COS were praying. Could this be another coincidence or was there something else going on just like the letter from my in-laws? I would have to consider this later, but for me it seemed that those things to think about were piling up at a fast and furious rate.

My musings were interrupted when I became aware that Carson was calling the police commander at the Concert Hall with the same instructions and notifying the human resource people at both sites that he needed the name and addresses of any students working in the buildings ASAP. I nodded to myself and was glad that Carson had moved on as my thoughts had wandered.

CHAPTER 15

Life Saviors Become Death Givers

It took the police three hours to remove all the fire extinguishers and process them for traces of Sarin gas. The initial results found that eight fire extinguishers, four at each place contained traces of the gas. I joined Christian, Nick, and Carson in watching as the lab techs carefully took apart and examined these eight extinguishers.

The techs, in conjunction with a local fire inspector, found very small changes to the interior structure, a tighter seal and a small chip not usually found in extinguishers. We suspected this chip was the probable trigger as it had a built-in receiver tied to a specific radio frequency, limited only by its range. This led us to suspect that someone in each building with a small radio transmitter had released the Sarin gas. That person would have to be in close proximity to the receivers leading us to suspect that the perps might be among the victims. Carson ordered an immediate search for any staff in the building.

I understood that finding someone with a small transmitter was going to be difficult under the circumstance. The transmitter could be hidden in a pen or a broach. A thorough study to find a transmitter directly connected to the fire extinguishers would be time consuming at best. But it was a start.

What little we could determine from the victims was that the problems started after the intermission, when the orchestra began playing the more religious Christmas music. This deepened the idea in my mind that this was an assault on the American dream, life in the U.S., the Great Satan and the Judeo-Christian values found so prevalently in the minds of so many.

I called Earnest to tell him my thoughts and was surprised that the COS had been thinking along the same lines. We discussed in detail upcoming events of national importance, now possible targets. Earnest indicated he would have the FBI; DHS and the CIA begin to look for patterns in the future that might suggest other targets. We both agreed this would be productive and hopefully help prevent any more attacks.

I returned to Carson's office to find the man on the phone with his Chief. Carson nodded and held up one finger. After hanging up, Carson shook his head, saying, "They have found two young men, one at each site, dead from the gas. One is a student from Great Britain and the other from Slovenia. They were considered good employees by both supervisors, quiet and industrious. There has been no indication that they might do something of this sort but no one seems to know much about them. They pretty much kept to themselves. We will begin a look into their past for anything suspect. Right now, we know nothing at all. This is really frustrating. I know you have seen this kind of thing in war zones but this is Boston! This is the U.S.! They seem to always be one step ahead of us!"

I nodded, saying, "It is true they seem to be in charge of things but they will make a mistake eventually. They always do and then we will catch them, maybe in the act, at least I hope so. In the meantime, let's concentrate on what we do know. Someone with a lot of help managed to plant those extinguishers in the two sites. Do we know who inspects them and how often?"

Carson shook his head but stated, "No, not now, but we will soon. I will make sure!"

"Good." I took a deep breath, "The sooner we know that, we can then deduce the rest. Also, can they check any entrances to the buildings for doors opening at odd times?'

"I would think so, it is all done by key stroke and maybe we can get a fingerprint but so many employees use the system it might not be helpful. We can determine if anyone entered the building at a time not consistent with normal work hours. I'll have my Sergeant check on that also. The forensic techs can check the doors for fingerprints as soon as possible. I'll tell them to check all these things and make sure no one messes with them until checked. Let me get on that, your people are still on site, right?"

I nodded. I called Christian. "Where are you now? Ok, in the building. Can you, Marcus or Jeremy move to the building's security office and check the records for doors opening at any odd times in the last week? I'm thinking that the extinguishers were brought into the building in that time frame. Carson is checking with Boston Fire Department (BFD) to see how often and when the last full inspections of them were done. I will call Dan and have him do the same. I hope this will give us a time frame for the attackers set up time. Carson is also checking with HR in both places about a couple of student workers found at each site that might be plants. Let me know if you find anything out of the ordinary, ok?"

"Sure thing, talk to you later!"

I felt in my heart that we might be on to something with these investigations. I was really beginning to think that prayer thing might be a big help. But questions still swirled in my mind.

Two hours later, the word was in. Two employees found dead on site, one in each building, were roommates and lived a short distance away. Their identities pegged them as students from foreign countries. They were also supposedly in the country to study engineering but local police were on their way to check their apartment. The local apartment manager had been contacted to meet them there. In the hours that had passed, seven more people had died, two of them children.

CHAPTER 16

Tracking Down the Devil's Henchmen

As Christian and Nick joined me, I commented, "The last full inspection was five days ago and everyone of them passed inspection. But, with these minute internal changes, it might be hard to nail down. Carson has been a big help and knows the ends and outs of who to contact with each possibility. He also had the authority to send the inspectors or lab people where we need them in short order."

Nick stated, "We don't have any solid leads in the how and when the fire extinguishers were brought into the buildings. We looked at the time scans for both buildings and saw one time three nights ago now where someone on the inside opened each of the employee doors briefly and it looked like about an hour and a half before it was briefly opened again from the inside. There is no sure way to tell who did it in either place."

I spoke quietly, "It seems we can deduce the time, after that last full inspection, but "the Who" is still a mystery. I am betting the two students found dead will be part of the answer but we still have to determine where the extinguishers came from. They were made specially to carry the

Sarin gas; it was only necessary to make very small changes to these eight but it took specialized skill to do that. We need to find out what company provided the extinguishers in the first place and when and to where they were originally shipped."

Carson entered the room in a rush with papers in his hand. I can tell you "The Who" now. My team sent to the student employee's apartment found signs of Islamic adherents in their space but more than that, they found that the two, or whoever is paying for them, had rented a small storage room on the same floor. In it, they found the regular fire extinguishers from both buildings, a table for working on them and signs of protective equipment. The techs are examining this room more closely for fingerprints as well. We are also checking the identifying numbers on these extinguishers with the original invoices to see if these were the ones delivered to the theaters. The apartment manager remembered that several deliveries were made to the young men last month. We will be able to follow up on those on Monday unless you can expedite that with your connections."

The three of us looked at each other and Nick spoke, "I can do that, Homeland can call up pretty much anyone on short notice in the case of national interest. I will get on that now." And he strode off, phone in hand.

I thanked and congratulated Carson for the good work of his men. "It has been a privilege to see your team move so quickly in this mess. We will get to the bottom of it eventually but these people have the means and the ways to move quickly. That is why time is so important."

Carson nodded and then added, "I hate that this has happened and my men are furious, I would almost hate it if one of them ran into one of the perps anytime soon.

Thinking of those children, and adults, but especially the kids, makes me sick to my stomach. I have a five-year-old at home and I shudder to think of anyone facing this but a kid?"

Christian laid a hand on Carson's shoulder and said, "I also have kids at home and this is really beyond understanding. But I have seen and read so much on these fiends use of children as weapons or pawns that it is useless to do anything but to try and find them."

The whole area dropped into a morose silence and then, one of the younger patrolmen, spoke, "so then let's roll!" With his words the whole room moved into action, grabbing phones or moving out to their beats.

The whole area became a beehive of activity. Homeland Security involvement allowed the people with proper clearances to chase down the shipping records of the few remaining fire extinguisher manufacturing companies based in the US. Nick's phone rang and he got the latest update. At last, one operator claimed to have found the closest one to Boston and after some quick coordination sent Nick PDFs of the shipping documents. Carson called his men to verify the serial numbers on the extinguishers they had found and the match was complete. A company in Minneapolis, Minnesota was the shipping company.

Several hours later, during a VTC with the team, DHS and the COS, a DHS agent reported, "We dug further into the fire extinguisher company's history. We found that it had been a supplier for the Boston area for years as a family-owned company but about 18 months ago, they sold it to a foreign company for a lot of money. Then about six months ago, that company sold it quickly for a large loss." Everyone's eyebrows raised, little red flags rising in our mind.

Earnest smiled, "This is a great clue; let's focus on this foreign company and the two students. I think this may be our first big break! I will call State; they can probably handle the students faster than anyone else. Keep up the good work and let me know what else you find."

Everyone's answer was a quiet, "Yes, Sir!"

As the night wore on, the officers all took a short break to eat and drink more coffee but their hearts were in the investigation and no one wanted to waste a moment. The work focused on the two young men found dead. It was hard to find information in the middle of the night but it did not stop anyone in Boston or Washington from trying.

As morning rose over the Boston Harbor the hunt continued but now, they could contact those who might have the answers they were looking for...shipping companies, storage places, the University Presidents, and anyone else they could think of on this solemn Christmas Day. The work overnight had the addresses and phone numbers listed carefully in order for the most likely answers.

All the Boston policemen fanned out in specific order to cover the places as quickly as possible. The young patrol officer was elated to find the shipping company located near the attack sites. The owner, a bit grumpy to be awakened so early on Christmas Day, met him at his office as quickly as he could after the officer explained the reason for his call.

As he poured over his invoices for the past months, he kept saying, I remember something strange but I can't tie it down." He was growing more frustrated as he went down the last two months.

"At last, here is that strange invoice. I knew something struck me odd at the time but it wasn't something I thought was significant.

The police officer, smiled and said, "Can I get a copy of that invoice?" The shipping company owner complied readily. After getting a copy of it, the police officer rushed back to headquarters. Within 15 minutes of getting back, Christian and I were handed a copy of the invoice by the lead investigator.

They reviewed it carefully and immediately sent a copy to the FBI with a request for an initial investigation by the Minneapolis office. We then called Ernest with the latest updates and after two more days digging in the trenches, we flew back to Huntsville to await any further developments.

CHAPTER 17

The Chill of Searching for Death

Christian and I shivered in the cold wind and snow as they exited the plane at the Minneapolis-Saint Paul International airport. It was a great deal colder than the Huntsville International airport we had flown from just hours ago. Alabama was cold by Alabama January standards but nothing like this upper mid-western city. Scurrying into the terminal they followed the directions in the note emailed to them from the Lead FBI Agent. It directed them to the Armed Forces Services Center on the mezzanine level of Terminal 1 and there they found an FBI agent awaiting them at the entrance.

George Gregory, a tall black man, spoke, "This was our least obvious way of connecting with you without creating any attention. Getting to the headquarters can be a bit hard, especially in the winter when the roads can be treacherous. I was sent to get you to Headquarters as quickly as possible."

Christian and I both nodded and smiled in thanks. We hurried out of the terminal and into the parking deck where Gregory had secured a parking space near the entrance. The ride was fairly lengthy and the roads did hold a number of hazards along the way.

Arriving at the Headquarters on the Freeway Boulevard in a suburb of Minneapolis, we were greeted by the Head Agent, Charles Williamson. He welcomed us with coffee and sandwiches since their arrival was late afternoon and we would be in the building for some time. We were delighted with the specialty sandwiches and coffee as we had only grabbed a snack in order to be on time for the plane.

As we ate, Williamson brought us up to date; "We have been alerted to your investigative needs and have been able to acquire a list of current and past employees of the Talent Fire Equipment Company. There was some confusion since the company has changed hands twice in the last year. The Talent family had owned it since its beginning in the early 1900's until last March when the grandson sold it at a huge profit and then in September it was sold again for a large loss. This caused a bit of chaos in the paperwork but the current owner was able to locate all the necessary names and addresses with the help of some of the older employees. There were a number of men who worked at the company during the second owner's time but they were all short time employees. One, a Martin Waith, was employed for several years and rose to an associate manager position. However, shortly before Christmas, he and his whole family disappeared without a trace; right after the latest owner took over. There was not so much as a fingerprint in the house the family lived in and we haven't heard anything to give us a clue as to where they went. They just disappeared. And we have also been unable so far to identify the interim owners. Another man, a logistical manager, who handled most of the shipping also left with no clues to his whereabouts. He was described as eccentric, rather Nordic looking and extreme in his need for accuracy for the shipments. Every bit of information we get just muddies the picture more!"

I smiled, "We know that feeling but I think we can help. Let me get the team's analysts on this and it may become much clearer. We have been chasing 'ghosts' since the 10/10 attacks and have a small amount of success but nothing else. This disappearance of a whole family with a name to go with it may be another small bit in the picture. Have you obtained any DNA or other physical identifiers on any of these people?"

Williamson looked through his notes and said, "We do have a DNA sample on Martin Waith but none of the others. No DNA unfortunately for the logistics guy. It doesn't appear he was even asked to do that."

"Well, it might come in handy sometime; I hope not too soon/long," I assured him, "I'm going to call my boss now and perhaps we can ask for a visit tomorrow?"

"Probably, the owner has been most cooperative, we can arrange for you to talk with some of the older employees who have been around since before the grandson took over. It's all been a bit unnerving for them and they remember a lot since it created a lot of change in their lives over a short period of time. I'll call first thing tomorrow morning."

I excused myself for a quick call to Earnest to update him on what we had found. "We have a couple of new names for research, Earnest. The Talent Fire Equipment Company, last owner, John Talent, a Martin Waith, who worked at the company and then he and his whole family disappeared around Christmas last year, no traces at all, sound familiar? Another man, the logistical manager, in charge of all the company shipping also quit and disappeared, don't have a name as yet. We are planning to visit the company tomorrow or as soon as possible. I would be willing to bet that that Ferris Conglomerate will show up somewhere in the first sale of the company. I think the pattern is pretty plain. When we have talked with the employees, I'll let you know anything else we learn."

Earnest Trowbridge gave a light shout of Praise, saying, "I think you and Christian have done well so far, you recognize the pattern. I did ask the FBI Director to alert the Field Office that we were interested in Fire Equipment companies and it looks like they have done a stellar job. I had the FBI Director notify them and to say that two specialists would be arriving to further the investigation. They do know it has to do with the Boston mess at Christmas. I'll look forward to hearing from you, God Bless."

I muttered a quiet, "Thanks, you too," and we hung up.

Returning to the conference room where our talks had taken place, I found Christian and Williamson having a rousing talk about football and the past season and the coming Super Bowl. They were primed and ready for a late supper and I joined in with laughter. All the messes in the world, but we could always talk football!

The next morning Williamson called the hotel to inform me, "I've set up a visit to the fire equipment company at 11 and then we can discuss whatever else you think is relevant. I don't know much else in this area; it has certainly been quiet especially since Christmas. You may have more knowledge than I do since you have been on more than one investigation. The Director said you two were part of a spearhead team to investigate everything that has happened. I'll see you about 10 and then we will go to the company. There aren't really any others in this area, a couple of small operations that do repairs but they also work with that company for obtaining parts."

"See you then," I responded. I turned to Christian, "that was Williamson; we are to be at his headquarters about 10 and at the company by 11. He says there aren't any other companies that make the extinguishers but some smaller operations that repair some. We may want to talk with them as well, as long as we are here. What do you think?"

Christian nodded, "Might as well be thorough but I don't see a repair shop doing the extent of work required for that attack. We might learn some names, though."

I nodded, glancing at my watch, it was 10 in Washington and I called Earnest. I was put straight through to the COS. "Good morning, John, what is your status there?"

I brought him quickly up to date and told him we were considering going to the local repair shops for possible information. "We should be done around three unless these shops are really far apart but I'll still call you with any information when we are done, unless it would be too late?"

"No, call whenever you are done. It is only an hour difference and I haven't been getting to bed very early anyway. I have the analysts working on the names you gave me last evening but this Ferris thing is always carefully hidden so I am not surprised we haven't nailed down anything yet, it is still early in the process. Talk with you soon, God Bless!"

I quietly responded with my now usual, "And you also, Sir."

We caught a cab to the headquarters and arrived at five till ten and strode into the Field Agent's waiting area. Williamson was waiting and we went to the car pool area and left for the company.

Half an hour later, we pulled up to the large brick building that had surely been standing for more than a century but appeared to be under some renovation. We looked it over and then entered through the large entrance and spoke with the guard.

Williamson told the guard, "We have an appointment with the owner." After a quick check of his list, the guard called and announced that the FBI people were here. He nodded to the elevator and said, "They are on the mezzanine floor and will meet you there."

It was a short ride during which Christian observed, "Sort of smells like a gun or bullet place. All the metal and chemicals." Neither of us commented.

CHAPTER 18

Source of the Extinguishers from Hell

The man that met us was about 55, balding and showing a small paunch but seemed friendly enough. "I only bought this place about 3 months ago from some big manufacturing concern but they just seemed to have decided that this wasn't for them. I don't know what they paid for it but it was a steal for me. I have a similar company in Illinois but it serves more of the mid-west and to have the door open to the east coast was a great big deal for me. Just what is it you need to know, Agent Williamson told me you would like to speak with some of the older employees? Is something wrong?"

I spoke up, "No sir, we are just trying to follow up on some leads in an ongoing investigation to the attacks in Boston. We are covering all possible leads."

"Horrid mess, I would sure like to get some of those... uh, oh, whatever. That Christmas mess was just too much," his voice trailing off as they hurried down the short hallway to his office.

We chose to not say anything but followed the man who seemed to be in a hurry.

In the office, I asked, "May we please check out the paperwork regarding your purchase of this company?"

He had it ready for us on his desk in a manila folder. Handing it to me, he said, "I sure don't understand what this has to do with all these attacks" but then fell silent. I could feel his eyes searching us for any clue as to what the meaning of this visit was, but I took my time reading the documents all the way through. The Charleston Manufacturing Company was the name given as the seller.

"Were any of the sellers at the closing?"

"Oh, no, it was just their lawyers, they were out of the country and the lawyers had power of attorney. Was something wrong with the sale?" he asked with a worried look.

"No, you have been more than helpful and the contract work is perfectly legal. Our main need now is to talk with your employees. Would now be a good time?"

"Yes, that is why I set this as the time, most will be on lunch break and you can talk with them in the small office just next to mine. Do you want to see them all at once, or one at a time?"

"One at a time for now, we may want to speak with all of them when we are done. We will try not to interfere with their work schedules too much. Thank you for your cooperation."

An hour and a half later, I sighed, murmuring to Christian. "No one seems to know much more than we already knew; this Waith guy sure kept to himself and didn't make many friends. We just have one more to talk with and then I guess we are done. You have any thoughts?"

"No, it is frustrating to find so little information, we've talked with ten?"

"Actually, eleven, the one on the way up is the twelfth. He has however been here the longest. The owner said he was involved in a technical glitch and will be right on up. I'm afraid this has been a bust for new information after the names we got last evening."

A knock on the door captured their attention and then it opened, a grizzled head peaked in and said, "You ready for me?"

"Yes, indeed. Come on in," I looked down at my list of names," Mr. Douglas."

"No need for that mister business; always just been Douglas for the thirty-five years I've been working here. What can I help you with?"

"Nice to meet you, Douglas. We are trying to tie up any loose ends in the attacks in Boston and there is strong evidence that the group used fire extinguishers in the attacks and this company is one of the largest distributors of extinguishers for the north east, we would like to hear your take on all of it.

"Terrible what happened in Boston, all those people, especially the kids. Didn't know that they used extinguishers, hope they didn't come from here. What exactly do you need to know? I have worked the floor for nearly twenty years; don't really know anything about shipping."

"We are assuming that you knew this fellow, Waith, uh, Martin Waith."

"Sort of, quiet fellow, hard worker but not pushy, you know? I think he was from the Middle East somewhere but never heard him speak about it. Know he had two or maybe three kids, only because he had to leave work, maybe five, six, years ago for a birth. Other than that, don't know much. Hum, but toward the end, he did bring in some other guys, 'all looking like him and they seemed to hang out together, pretty standoffish if you ask me. But they worked ok and then they quit abruptly and left. Never saw any of them again, even in town. Now, the logistics man, he came in after third John sold the place. Didn't see that coming, I'll tell you. But he was different, he looked like a lot of folks in Minnesota, sort of Nordic, you know. But he stayed in his office, pretty picky about things, or so I heard. Some of the fellows were a bit put off by him but he definitely made the shipping more efficient. But he quit also, about Christmas time, just like Waith, but he hadn't been here but a couple of months. You might ask the men in the shipping department about him. It was all very confusing, the sale out of the blue and then to turn around just after the Christmas, well, end of the year, shipments were sent out, and we got another owner. I hope this one turns out to be here for longer than a few months. It sure is disconcerting having a new boss. Wasn't like that when I started here, only eighteen I was, but the old man, Talent, he was a John and so was his son. That's why we called the grandson third John. Kind of our joke, you know. Well, don't know if that is any help but I sure hope you government folks figure it all out. Things seem to be getting out of hand, if you were to ask me."

I smiled at the talkative soul. I had learned a bit and was happy to tell the gentlemen that he had been, "more than helpful, really, more than helpful."

The older man nodded and left the room with a parting shot, "You fellows catch them bad guys, you hear?"

Christian and I had a laugh when they were sure the man was out of hearing range. "What a character!" I said and Christian chortled, "Yes, indeed, I guess we have our marching orders!"

But our mood lasted only a moment. "I think we need to move on to the shipping department. Perhaps someone there will remember this strange Nordic man and what he actually did" I murmured. Christian just nodded.

After notifying the owner, they moved to the shipping department. These workers were a lot younger than most they had already spoken with and so the hope of finding out anything helpful went down. But in speaking with the newest logistical fellow, they were in for a surprise.

"I've been going over all these shipping records at the owner's request. I found something odd at the end of the year report. While the numbers were accurate and tally with the other years, the number from our shipper did not. They reported two boxes sent to a strange address in Boston that is not a company or user and it was never resolved that I can find. The numbers in our records don't show those shipments and never appear in any other records before last year. Sending out our extinguishers is pretty routine and looking back 6 or 7 months, I can't find anything that matches that difference. Sometimes there will be a difference of a box or two but not this kind of difference. It's a bit of a puzzle but since the people who worked this aren't available, I can't account for the discrepancy. I called the number I found for the address and it appears to be an apartment house or so the manager said. He did recall getting two boxes for one of the tenants. But only after the police came to check on those tenants, did he think it odd. The two tenants have disappeared and no one has even checked to see about them."

I, looking straight at Christian, asked, "How many extinguishers are normally sent in a box?

"Four, any more would be too heavy one person to handle."

Christian and I took a deep breath. Eight was the exact number used in the Boston attacks on Christmas Eve. We thanked the young fellow after getting the odd address, and returned to the owner's office. We filled him in on what they could tell him and left.

As we got into the car, the FBI Lead Agent Williamson was ripe with enthusiasm. He had noticed the deep sighs and said, "OK, what can you tell me about all that? I saw the looks on your faces and the owner might have missed it but I could tell that the information in the shipping department was meaningful to you."

I had known this was coming and decided to tell the man. He had been extremely helpful. "Well, what we know for sure is that two students working in Boston, one at the Boston Pops Concert Hall, and the other at the Opera Theater are now the suspected trigger men of those attacks. They lived at the apartment house at the address given by the shipping department. Both appeared to have died in the attacks but as other employees had also died, they weren't necessarily suspects, but this presents a very different scenario from our initial thinking. We had no proof that they were involved in the attacks but now knowing_that the eight extinguishers being sent to their apartment building sheds a whole new light on our investigation. The Boston police did visit the apartment after the attacks but other than them concealing their Muslim faith, there was no proof that they were directly involved. This changes that entirely and we will have to investigate their backgrounds a great deal closer.

The Boston Police Department found a room with the regular fire extinguishers but the apartment manager could not definitely tie it to them. He said it was rented as a storage space by a company, which he did think weird, but the money came regularly and he didn't think much about it. He was devastated to learn the regular fire extinguishers were in his building after the attacks. So, there you have it."

"My God, oh, my God!" was all we got out of Williamson. We tended to agree with him.

The call to Earnest took place during dinner at the White House but Earnest jumped up with the barest of excuses to take it. He was jubilant but also taken aback to learn their news. "I will have the analysts get right on those two. How about that for success? I'll inform the President and let you know what we find. Thanks, and God Bless."

I murmured my thanks and you too.

Christian smiled.

CHAPTER 19

The Realtor of Death Arrives: Houston, TX

The Imam in charge at the Mosque where Charles Arndell/ Tumbrel Arrow was staying kept Fletcher Cordell, "The Ghost", updated on a daily basis using Facebook. They used a code agreed upon to hide the meaning of their messages. This kept Fletcher aware of what was going on with his operative, and the plans status. The Ghost gave the Imam his latest directive for the operation and ended the session.

Staying at the Mosque, I, Charles Arndell, kept saying the name in my head over and over to set it in my mind, found myself with some time on my hands, decided to drive around in the area to become aware of the possibilities for our next mission. Wandering down I-45 towards Galveston, I took note of all the processing plants for crude oil situated along the highway. I began to consider how to execute the plans given to me by The Ghost. I would look at all the small towns in the surrounding vicinity, seeking Allah's direction.

At the Mosque that evening, I reviewed maps of the area and found a couple of possibilities, Pasadena and Bay Town. The next morning arrived clear and hot, and I drove toward Pasadena using I-610. Surprised at how quiet the streets of Pasadena were, I finally took a left turn and found myself driving into a small suburb with the astonishing name of Bycycle.

While Pasadena was larger, Bycycle sported a number of closed and/or abandoned business sites. A quick circle through two small residential areas showed me a depressed economic situation, which would fit our needs. Although possible work was available at the oil refineries, the town's other businesses seemed decimated by the lack of customers. The area needed the supporting businesses like groceries, restaurants, gas stations, and such. I could take care of that part. I had access to plenty of money and return on the investment didn't matter to my backers. They were using the money to advance their Jihad against the Great Satan.

Continuing my search, I drove down I-610 and turned north on SR-146, and finding my way to Baytown. While seeing similar possibilities, I noted that Baytown was not on the main freeways and therefore harder to access. It also didn't have easy access to the local shipping lanes. After seeing all this, I made an initial decision on a possible way forward and turned toward home.

That evening, the Imam called me over to finalize our plans. Finding a base of operations for jihadists in the area was officially my first order of business. I was ready and already knew where I was going. I felt a sense of joy for Allah providing a quick solution. Now, I would associate myself with a realtor in the Houston/Sugar Land area and the rest would be easy.

The next morning, I drove to the Clinton Park suburb in the south east Houston metropolitan area. I drove the length of Clinton Park Street until I spied a real estate office on the corner of Clinton Park and North Carolina streets. Entering the small office, I took note of the disheartened looking man seated at a desk in the back of the otherwise empty office. It was perfect for my needs and purposes.

Randy Price, looked up as the door opened jingling from the bell hanging above the door. He was hopeful as he saw a well-dressed young man enter. Maybe, just maybe, here was someone who would buy a house, or well, anything. His town, stagnating, had no hope and no-one believed anyone could change anything. Most of the work he currently handled was foreclosures for the banks, not very lucrative work. He and his wife were just making it on his small income. While the oil industry was active, the drastic drop in the price of gas depressed the local economy. Everyone was just getting by, if at all.

Randy said, "How can I help you?" Trying to sound encouraging to me as he rose, reaching out to shake my hand. I liked the firm handshake and I could feel his optimism. This changed as I introduced myself as a fellow realtor. Randy said. "I have no work to offer." His voice moving to a sad tone. But my reaction was totally unexpected.

I, seeing the shower of emotions crossing Randy's face, hastened to explain. "My job is to find an area for a philanthropic consortium of financiers I work with to see what we can do to help the area recover. The consortium is involved in many places around the country and recently completed several projects. We began to notice this area's needs and they sent me ahead to find realtors with whom we could work to help reestablish viable communities. They see the oil industry making a recovery and wish to finance some endeavors to build community and of course make some money as well. Your office caught my attention as it is similar to ones we've worked with before." I then asked Randy: "Are you interested in learning more?"

Randy stumbled back down into his worn chair with a thud; wondering if this was a dream, but readily asked for more information. I smiled. I was ready with my story of a group of financial wizards who liked to take a philanthropic stance and have some tax write-offs to boot. I had developed this whole scenario with the help of my handlers. It was amazing how well it sounded and worked for us. As I completed my story, I recognized the hope building on Randy's face. I felt sure I had found my 'partner'.

Randy asked: "What about the financial side of all this? He said: "All the local banks are pretty well tapped out and all the larger institutions are leery of messing with this small of an endeavor."

I nodded, no fool this one. I stated: "Our Company is well aware of the situation and we have separate banking sources." I added: "We are able to handle anything that comes up and they have authorized me to act on my own unless it is over two million dollars."

I smiled again. I asserted: "We know that this area is quite depressed, thus the reason we want to help. We have business associates interested and ready to come into this area, bringing businesses with them. We have researched this area and we have the money, people, and the businesses ready to move. We desire local participation in the set up. With your help, the community will be less likely to fight the businesses moving in. This success will encourage more businesses to move into the area. We want to use local workers for all the businesses and get locals also involved in improving the housing for Company families who would move to the area. This will encourage locals to open small businesses creating a local market and money flow. This is a building process to revitalize the county."

Randy appeared energized, and was game to begin. He mumbled under his breath, "This couldn't hurt anyone and it sure would help a lot of my neighbors. I can't wait to get home and tell Sarah about it. I can reassure her that it soon would be different." He had a spring in his step as he locked the door of his office and started his car saying, "What a difference a few hours could make!"

Little did Randy know that he had just made a bargain with a devil, a nice-looking, well-spoken devil, but a devil none the less. For now, he was thrilled to be the bearer of good news for a change. Looking a gift horse in the mouth wasn't his style and he sure wasn't going to turn this one down.

Sarah was preparing their dinner when he arrived and jumped when he shouted a greeting to her from the front door. She turned from her simple preparations and stared at this man who once again resembled the young man she had married. She hoped for the best.

But Sarah was totally unprepared for the news Randy poured out as she finished their dinner. He was so excited that she said nothing. But in her spirit, she felt a check. What did that mean? But her heart won and she said nothing, vowing to pray about the whole thing. It sounded so good, what was not to like in their situation, the town's situation? She would pray.

Randy assured her the young man would be back ready to begin this new endeavor on Monday. He was so happy he agreed to go to church with Sarah on Sunday. Perhaps the Lord hadn't forgotten them after all. He had no clue, but right now in the present, he was more than excited. He was willing to give it all a chance.

CHAPTER 20

Death Finds a New Home: Bycycle, Texas

I showed up promptly on Monday, appearing chipper and excited. I had received the go ahead from the Imam. Randy was so happy to see me, he almost hugged me. I stated that, I had begun to worry over the weekend that I had been a figment of his imagination or a horrible joke.

Since the "Consortium" had taken care of all the necessary legal requirements of setting me up with a realtor license, it was easy to get integrated into Randy's office. We spent the morning taking care of these issues and then had a nice lunch at the local restaurant, the only one still open. It was the place most of the town visited to see each other and catch up on the local gossip. Most could only afford coffee, but the owner, a long-time resident, understood. Occasionally, even he wondered how long he would be able to stay open, but until absolutely necessary, he would stay open to offer himself and his neighbors hope.

As they returned to the office, I requested: "Can we take a tour of the town?" He agreed and gave me the low down on each area as we drove through the neighborhoods. I wanted to hear what Randy said and he was more than helpful during the ride, talking about 'what sort of people lived where' in the town. I was personally interested in houses for my people and any business sites that could help hide the true purposes of my group from the locals.

I kept from Randy that the new comers would keep to themselves and practice their religion quietly, coming together in private homes behind closed doors. The "Consortium" used this technique to prevent any awkward questions about who they were or their purposes. But the fact was that with the money we would bring into this area, the desperately needed income would mask initial questions. It stood to reason that few locals would have a problem with the new people as the local economy improved. The leadership had found that this method helps ease the transition of their people.

I chose a small residential area on the north side of town for my first move. I told the Imam of my decision and began the process of getting the legal information on the foreclosures in that section. I visited the courthouse and gathered the names of the banks holding the mortgages along with the names of the current owners. I would target these homes as a good faith gesture to the locals cementing the idea that new businesses would indeed be coming to town. I had studied the town's businesses, both past and present, sending this information on to the Conglomerate.

The Conglomerate studied the official information but relied on firsthand information from me before choosing who and what businesses they would open first. First the construction foremen for renovating properties would arrive and hire as many locals as possible to build good will. Then we would begin setting up a small manufacturing facility for making something, maybe furniture, maybe fishing or boating stuff since the water was so close. All the earlier research provided direction for the work.

I constantly kept The Ghost informed and received directions though the Imam. I kept my ears open to what the locals talked about. I would have to depend on Randy to introduce me at first but I had learned in Iowa how to insert myself into the business and political community.

The plan underway, I decided that perhaps I too should move to an apartment or small house in Bycycle. That way, I would be close to the action and able to keep tabs on what was happening. It had worked well when I did this is Iowa.

I found a small house on the east side of town, about one thousand square feet with a small yard. I didn't care for yard work and liked apartments better but I wanted it to appear that I was there for the long haul. After all, it was larger than the one I'd grown up in with my five siblings and parents. The Ghost approved the purchase of the small house and it did not take long for the owners to accept my offer for more than it was worth.

In the meantime, I allowed Randy to take care of the business part, including receiving the commissions for the sales. This set well with Randy and cemented our relationship with me to the point that he did not ask questions unless directly business related.

With The Ghost's blessing, I hired a local decorator to furnish my house to start stimulating the local business contacts. My taste was simple and clean and it was an easy move in after closing. I settled in, bringing my prayer rug in after the final walk though. Noticing a neighbor mowing his grass, I offered the man a generous sum to mow mine while he did his own. The neighbor, already struggling for money, accepted at once. I won hearts with these moves. I was ready, the town was ready, and all would begin quickly.

The first business men arrived two weeks after I completed my establishment in the community. We met at my house on the first night. The 'owner' of the Charleston Manufacturing, actually a representative of the Farris Consortium, looked over the small house, commented favorably and told me to buy more like it for their future workers.

The 'owner' emphasized to me that the plan was to hire local people to do the repair work and to pay them well. My final instruction from my visitors was to focus on those whose homes were in foreclosure. Most were still living in the homes since the bank preferred that the houses not be left empty. This would give hope to the men chosen to work for the construction company to modernize the houses.

The men asked me about the name of the area out of sheer curiosity. I was prepared. I had asked Randy about the unusual name for a community. Randy had laughed hardily.

I regaled them with the story. "Apparently the man who first bought the land was very old fashioned, and didn't believe in or trust those 'new fangled gasoline cars' and wouldn't let one on his property. He rode a bicycle everywhere and so did his family. The area people nicknamed it Bicycle and it stuck. When the man's grandson inherited the property, he chose to change the spelling to emphasize the unusual name. He finally sold some of the property during the Depression and that's how Bycycle became a town. It makes a great story and the locals were just tickled to live here and be eccentric!"

I shook my head and laughed, saying to my mentors, "There is just no explaining these people!"

The next morning, I took the men on a tour of the town to determine a place for the manufacturing site. On the outskirts of town, we found a huge building that had been part of a small manufacturing complex. It had been a machine shop and seemed the perfect choice. It was far enough out of town not to be seen as a nuisance but close enough to allow the workers easy transport to and from work.

Within a month, all the paper work was done and the building officially belonged to the Farris Conglomerate under the name Charleston Manufacturing. The offer had been substantial enough to bring the owners of the run-down parcel to the table quickly.

The first few men began to arrive over the next month, one or two at a time moving seamlessly into the fabric of the town. They 'bought' homes since some brought families with them.

As this was being done, some of the men in town, meeting at the local union hall, were talking. They discussed among themselves all the new men who were arriving with families in tow and bought the houses in town that had been in receivership for some time. Rumor had it that a lot of updated renovations were planned. Only one had any questions, which was, why did they all seem to be foreigners? He was told to stop looking a gift horse in the mouth and he quickly withdrew any vocal questions.

There was cautious hope that some of them would be hired to help with the work. Everyone hoped it was all a fact and not a dream. They all left the place with a slightly lighter weight on their shoulders. They felt there might be hope for their little town again.

About one week after the initial arrivals, the work began on the building to turn it into a first-class machine shop. The construction foreman hired a number of men from the town and hope soared. Some of the town's men began talking of restarting businesses they had run before the downturn in the area. This would also offer work for some of their wives which sparked a renewal spirit. People began to speak of the future with optimism.

The new people joined in at the school, the town council meetings, and at the local restaurant where folks had always gathered. The owner was thrilled; he had enough paying customers that closing down no longer haunted his thoughts. Not that the newcomers said or did much but appeared interested. This caused the town people to appreciate that even though they were instrumental in bringing new life to town, they weren't trying to take control. This was totally according to plan.

As life took on a new optimism, the young people stopped talking of moving to the bigger city area of Houston. It all seemed so good that the new comers were welcomed with warmth. They were bringing life back to Bycycle. No one paid much attention to the background of the newcomers; they were bringing life and that was AOK with everyone concerned. Things were looking up!

Only Randy's wife had questions but her husband and her neighbors were so overjoyed with the changes that she kept quiet and prayed a lot. She truly didn't understand the concern that almost ate at her spirit all the time. Her only peace came as she talked with God.

Her prayers were simple and direct. She was not unhappy about all these changes; she just told her Lord how much it meant to her and the town that they were looking forward again. But her spirit just couldn't settle down, something seemed so wrong. How did she deal with this other than coming to Him?"

Randy Price caught himself humming on his way to work. He was ecstatic. His thoughts kept acknowledging that this was helping his neighbors return to a real life of hope and joy. And the money that flowed into his office from all the Real Estate deals enabled him to move toward getting out of debt, maybe in the black again. His business was the most productive thing in town, except for the restaurant, and he thanked God everyday for Charles Arndell's arrival, sometimes actually singing praises in his car.

As the community of Bycycle became more active, more of my allies arrived, not in mass, still in small groups, one or two, sometimes three or four, all coming for The Charleston Company. Each arrival appeared to have specialized skills to work on the refurbishing of the town. Others opened stores where men and women from the town found work, a hardware store, a larger grocery, an updated drug store, and other shops that increased the sense of permanency.

We were quiet and non intrusive though welcomed by the locals. We took turns traveling to Houston on Friday for prayers at the Mosque. Those not going assembled at one of our residences and held private prayers so that the locals were totally unaware of these activities.

The men of the Charleston Manufacturing were diligent in doing the 'work' that appeared to have brought them to the area but hid their excitement for the real mission. The group sent out four small planes from the local municipal airport on regular flights to establish a working relationship and pattern with the airport managers and workers.

On the seventh day of the seventh month, the Imam in Houston relayed to The Ghost that everything was ready in Bycycle.

"They have responded with great enthusiasm to the orders. It has taken every bit of the seven months but the day is here. Everything is in place, people, supplies, and means. They brought small planes to the local municipal airport and established a working relationship with the managers and workers. They are ready, we await the final go ahead. Each has made his peace with his part in the mission and they stand at the ready."

The Ghost was more than pleased. He was somewhat superstitious about dates and the fact that this was the seventh day of the seventh month pleased him. He knew now that Allah had orchestrated all of this, 'praise be unto Him'.

This last scheduled Friday prayer service was attended by all the men who had come to Bycycle for this mission. Each of the four pilots gave a solemn testament to their faith and trust in Allah's plan and that this is what they had been born to do. The Imam spoke a blessing over all the men, each with a special part in this mission.

CHAPTER 21

God's Wrath from Above: Bycycle, TX

It was Monday, March 22nd and everyone was geared up for this mission, the pilots to meet in Paradise and the rest to move on as ordered. Only the equipment and goods in the machine shop and other businesses would remain as a question for the authorities and town's people to puzzle over. We felt good.

Sarah Price awakened with a heavy feeling of doom but did not share that with her husband. She shared it with her Lord and still felt the heaviness but not the doom. She continued in prayer during the morning as she worked about the house.

The airport manger, aware of the recent alerts by the FAA and his own questions about the foreign staffing of the Charleston Manufacturing noted a change in their flight plans. The company routinely sent out only one or maybe two of the planes on the same day. Sending all four planes within a short time span was so unusual that he decided to call the Sherriff.

"Edgar, that Charleston outfit, the one with all the foreign newcomers today have flight plans for all four of their planes to take off, within a short period of time. That is something that has never happened before. I know of no reason but my gut is telling me something out of the ordinary. They have been quiet, kept to themselves, and provided much needed work for good pay to so many, but I don't feel good about this. So, what are your thoughts on it?"

The Sherriff heard his friend out. "I understand your concern and I have that same uneasy feeling in my gut. Keep me posted on the activity, OK?"

"Sure enough" was his only answer.

The Sherriff acted on it. He called the Department of Homeland Security office in Houston. Maybe he'd look like a fool but after the October 10th attacks of last year, he was taking no chances. Better to look a fool than to be a fool.

Everyone sitting at the Monument Inn and Restaurant, which sits on the bluff overlooking the final short canal of the Houston channel system where it emptied into the Crystal Bay, were startled by a loud explosion at about 10:10 that same morning. The explosion caused the building's huge windows to shudder. Hurrying to the large bay-side windows, the employees and guests saw a large tanker easing its way around the almost ninety-degree turn from the Houston side. It was all normal, except for the huge black hole in its side. The ship swerved into the final turn listing to port and expelling burning fuel into the water. The curves in the canals create a Y shape turn for egress, one stem from the eastern refinery area and the other served the western side, coming from the greater Houston area.

Both accesses turned into this short canal to move into Galveston Bay, and then to the ocean. This is the main water outlet for all the transport traffic to reach international waters. It was also the way the vast amounts of refined oil were transported to world markets and also the only access in for ships carrying crude into the Houston area refineries. Houston is the largest home to refineries in the United States.

As the tanker began to roll over, a container ship coming from the eastern canal lumbered into place to enter the egress waters. The Container ship's Captain yelled for all stop but stopping such a large ship is neither easy nor quick. This one was had been slowing to make the easier turn from the east but seeing it was not going to stop before colliding with the tanker, the Captain tried to turn it into the western area. The ship turned slightly in the time it had but then floated into the tanker at mid section. This action pushed the tanker forward into the short canal and caused it to begin sinking. Meanwhile, the container ship lay across the meeting of the V section of the Y, effectively closing it off. The men of the tanker were abandoning the burning ship, swimming toward land. Those on the container ship also began to exit their ship. It was altogether possible that the tanker fire could spread to their ship as well.

Both Captains radioed the Port Authority reporting their situation and a Navy patrol started their way. Of course, they had the equipment to raise a sunken ship quickly but it would take some time and an investigation would delay the process. Houston's NCIS (Naval Criminal Investigations Service) team was also on the way and the local authorities commanded everyone involved to remain until questioned. At the moment, fire was consuming all the oil spilling into the water but a through cleansing would still have to be done. The Port Authorities notified the Department of Homeland Security (DHS) and the FBI. DHS passed the information up through channels and the President was briefed within half an hour.

As authorities struggled with the shipping mess, about noon, the first Charleston Manufacturing Company airplane took off. The other three planes took off about ten minutes apart. No one was concerned until about thirty minutes later when all four planes suddenly dropped off the radar screen at the local airport control tower.

The local tower notified the Department of Homeland Security and the FBI. DHS informed the higher commands adding the Sherriff's call to DHS earlier to the information. The oil spill was of paramount importance in some minds but the NCIS team was looking for the cause of the explosion on the tanker. The timing of the explosion coincidently happened at the worst possible moment, the lead agent didn't believe in coincidences.

While the channel mess was taking up a lot of attention, moments after the planes disappeared, a thunderous boom resounded across the area. Everyone in the Bycycle Air Traffic Control Tower heard the boom and saw the flames leap into the air near Pasadena only a few miles away. Concerned that a plane crash had occurred, the intensity of the flames and loudness of the explosion raised questions for the first responders. They considered that this might be a much worse event.

Within moments, a second and then a third blast were heard. Everyone now knew that just like on 9/11 after the second airplane strike that it wasn't an accident, this was without a doubt not mere plane crashes, but deliberate attacks in play. The Sherriff heard the booms and saw the flames climb to the limits of his vision. It had happened, a terrorist attack on his watch, he thought with horror. Within seconds of the last boom, the entire phone tree lit up and every phone in the office began ringing. The dispatch operator buzzed him.

He answered the first one confirming the awful news. The local fire department was reporting a massive fire at the Pasadena refinery and they were on route to the scene. The Fire Chief told him he had put out a call to the surrounding fire departments for assistance but every department in the area was now involved with the three different fires, all at oil refineries. Other first responders, already deploying to the Channels to help with the shipping mess, were now rushing to the new refinery fires. Someone in the Coast Guard or the Navy would have to handle the Channel mess; the local fire departments were overwhelmed. It was the perfect storm for emergencies.

About five minutes later, a fourth explosion was reported in the area near Baytown. Baytown police and fire were calling into the area police and fire departments, only to find out they too were on their own. The call went out from Houston for the counties across the state to send any assistance they could muster. The Texas Governor was already making calls for a declaration of a national emergency for Houston and the surrounding counties. He also made a call to the Texas National Guard, asking for assistance in road and traffic control and engineering unit help to the fire departments.

CHAPTER 22

Hell Raising: Pasadena, Texas

Television coverage out of Houston was up and running in about thirty minutes, they were reporting on both the situation in the channel and refinery fires. News reporters were claiming that eye-witness accounts reported that a small cargo plane crashed into the Pasadena Refinery on Red Bluff Road. The scene was still burning at such a high temperature that not even fire fighters could get close. The local Fire Chief claimed that the suspected damage and loss of life was high during a quick interview.

Meanwhile the police were hurriedly evacuating the housing areas around the refinery. Fortunately, it was the middle of the day and few people were at home. Those who were seemed disoriented. Most of them were in shock, appearing not to comprehend what had just occurred.

The Department of the Navy, using satellite imagery confirmed that four different refineries were burning white hot and also showed clearly the two ships stuck in the channel. This confirmation eliminated any doubts these were deliberate attacks. The question on everyone's minds was by whom? The Department of Homeland Security, FBI, and all the local first responders were moving onto the scenes. DHS and the FBI agents set up a combined base of operations in Pasadena, maintaining contact for command and control with their permanent offices in Houston. DHS immediately notified the President. The fires were at the four largest refineries in the Houston area and the impact to the oil flow across the nation and the world, making it a National Security, an economical, and ecological disaster.

The local news channels were reporting that the four refineries hit included the Baytown Refinery, the Galveston Refinery, the Beaumont Refinery, and of course the Pasadena Refinery and represented a large loss of life and ability to service the oil needs of the country.

Randy called his wife Sarah telling her to turn on the news. She stumbled back and fell on the couch, stunned at the news of the attacks at the four refineries. She immediately started praying for the families of those lost, and for the area's economic loss. She could feel her husband's devastation and sadness for the losses. He explained to her that he had tried to call Charles Arndell, the 'angel' who was to bring renewal to the area but couldn't reach him now. His initial fear was that he had been hurt during the attacks, or worse that Charles might have been killed, thus ending the possible rejuvenation of the community.

The COS and President Brooks got the call from the Texas Governor as they were watching the reports on CNN. Earnest, mumbled a quick prayer, during the conversation and listened to the Governor state he thought this was another terrorist attack, America was becoming a war zone. Earnest could see the frustration on President's Brooks face as he listened and told the Governor that he would put the whole power of the US Government into investigating this attack. Hanging up the phone, the President yelled at Earnest, saying, "Enough is enough, I want these criminals stopped!" Earnest nodded stating, "I will get moving on this right away!" God had answered his prayer; he had already decided to call the team. Calling me, he said, "Once more into the breach!" Earnest started the coordination for travel for the team and setting up briefings for the President and himself from the entire intelligence community led by the Director of National Intelligence (DNI).

With all regular air travel grounded coming in and out of the Houston area, we had to fly in on a military C-141 provided by the Air Force. During the flight, I passed out assignments in a process that was becoming all too familiar for our liking. Christian and I will go to the command post in Pasadena and start coordination. Tanya, should be there in a couple of hours as well, she caught a flight out of DC. Dan and Bill will cover the Baytown Refinery, Marcus and Jeremy; you cover the channel situation with your knowledge about ships. Nick, I need you to start your magic with Homeland Security and see what you can find out, that they may not be willing to share with just us peons.

CHAPTER 23

Controlling the Chaos: Pasadena, Texas Later the Same Day

At the central command post for the crisis, Christian and I, after some initial introductions, receive a briefing from several first responders. The most up to date information was from the first responders on the scene of the ship's accident. This pudgy officer, with a Texas drawl, said; "It was the first to happen and we had more time to survey the area. We talked with the staff at the Monument, they all told me that many of the sailors fleeing from the tanker stopped to watch their ship slowly turn over and float upside down in the water. But one waitress, Agnes," he said flipping through his notebook, "told me she saw someone running away. She said he disappeared into the bushes behind the Inn. She described him as youngish, covered in tattoos everywhere she could see. We put out an APB and are currently hunting for this person of interest." The On Ground Commander, seeing the quizzical looks, explained, "He's talking about the Monument Inn on the bluff overlooking the channel. It is a local gathering spot and it is right across the street from a San Jacinto Battleground Monument."

The next briefer was the lead FBI investigator from Houston area office. He spoke, "You probably already know what has been reported by the media, the only other possible clue was a local sheriff reported that the manager of a small airport near Bycycle, TX, called him to say he was disturbed by a change of flight habits of a group of foreign nationals."

I asked, "Do you know the name of the company associated with the pilots?" He replied, "Charleston Manufacturing." I wrote down the name as Christian and I exchanged glances with raised eyebrows remembering a similar name from Minneapolis. As soon as possible, we excused ourselves from the agent, and I called the COS, "Sir, there was a report of someone with a suspicion about a change in flight plans of a Charleston Manufacturing in Bycycle, TX. We were also told about a tattooed person leaving the scene of the tanker explosion has also raised our suspicions. The Authorities had been trying to monitor the movements of a group called MS-13, young men from Central America, who are part of a gang with a terrible record of criminal activities, murder by some as young as age 10. The tattoos were a symbol of gang membership. These youths had spilled into the country among all the 'children' arriving in mass during the spring and summer months. They have been shipped off around the country, leaving authorities annoyed and irate. It was impossible to track the where abouts of so many."

Earnest Trowbridge said, "I will institute an immediate background check." Everyone involved had a sinking feeling that somewhere in a long list of legal entities the name Farris Construction Company would emerge.

About a day and a half later, Earnest called me to inform us, "We found the Farris Construction Company or more precisely The Farris Conglomerate as a deeply hidden owner of the Charleston Manufacturing Company. The expressed purpose of the company was to make specialty parts for manufacturing tools that broke during work. This meant a lot of flying to take the parts to various legitimate companies."

"But on that day, the flights took off together with the simple but doubtful answer that the company had been extra busy with orders and had a number of parts to deliver. The whole endeavor had proved an ingenious cover for their flights, cleverly disguising their real purpose."

Christian and I chose to go to the supposed company that afternoon. Driven by an FBI agent, we arrived at the Charleston Manufacturing Company to find it abandoned with a minimal amount of equipment that seemed not to have been used in some time if at all. A search for the people who had worked there began immediately and like previously we found no-one, even the families were gone. Checking with the school, the children attending from that group had not come to school that day and the school could contact none of the families. Again, everyone involved seemed to have just vanished overnight.

The locals were mystified and afraid, with a growing feeling of betrayal filling them all. Most of them had been hired to work on refurbishing the homes the foreigners had bought. With each discovery of these homes also abandoned, the level of disappointment, horror, and anger grew. The locals began to realize that the promised improved economic situation was a hoax and their hopes dropped like a bucket into a deep well. They voluntarily told the authorities one after another that no local people had been hired to work at that facility. To everyone's dismay, no one had questioned it before, only excited by the prospect of an improved economic climate. But now this stood as a huge red flag in everyone's mind, the Sherriff painfully wondering at his own lack of curiosity.

In a quickly convened conference call, the President's COS and our team discussed all the known facts and it all added up to another win for the enemy. Earnest tasked Christian and I to begin a search for the person who had facilitated the renting and buying of properties in the area.

Christian and I had a small but clear picture of the 'Realtor' who worked in this capacity in Iowa. The picture had been in the locked file of the Real Estate owner's office where one Tumbrel Arrow had worked. He disappeared completely within days of the 10/10 attacks. The owner of the Realty Company where 'The Realtor' had reported him as a missing person but related to us that all trace of him had vanished but she still had the picture on one of her fliers listing the name and picture of all those working in her office. She also confirmed that this man had done all the work on the now abandoned sites where the terrorists had lived.

During the conference call, I informed the group of our findings. "After completing conversations with all the locals who had contact with the men of the machine shop, we expanded our search area and finally found the Real Estate office of Randy Price. He is completely undone, barely able to focus on our questions. But as we talked, he began to calm down and told us a familiar story of a handsome young man, not foreign looking at all, coming into his office with an offer that seemed too good to be true. With tears in his eyes, he now admits that it had been too good to be true. Christian asked for a description of this man."

Christian took up the story, "Randy gave a short, clear picture of a young man in perhaps his early thirties, blond hair, blue eyes, and wearing glasses. He gave his name as Charles Arndell and all his papers were in perfect order. Price had seen no reason to question his identity. Wearing very nice clothes and driving a high-end sedan with all the bells and whistles, his whole manner spoke of money and lots of it. He recalled that when he first met him, the man's hair had been darker, like a light to medium brown but had grown out a lighter color, not a silvery blonde, just a much lighter blonde.

Randy added the man spoke very clear English with a slight British accent but had all the American idioms down pat. Randy accepted him at face value and been ecstatic with the offer of help with the area's economic troubles. He told us that the man told him that he worked for a charitable organization that wanted to help depressed areas with economic input from worldwide donations. Randy had accepted this as the truth and now, what would happen to the people who had been hoodwinked, including himself? People, who had hoped again and now, were more depressed and very distressed over the outcome. When we showed him the picture of the Iowan Realtor, he slowly nodded. It was the same man without the glasses and with hair the color it had grown out as."

Everyone on the phone call remained quiet for a moment as they took in the news. This was terrible, the loss of life, livelihood, economic loss, and hope for thousands of Americans. How were they to proceed to counter this tragedy? Add to that the ecological damage, and much was riding on our actions now.

Earnest finally cleared his throat, saying in a quiet voice, "Efforts must redouble to find this man. He is a chameleon with the heart of a devil and seems to be in the vanguard of the enemy's work to destroy this nation in as many ways as possible. It will take months if not years to overcome the damage to our oil infrastructure. This means we must get our hands on him. I want all of you to combine forces in Texas to find him before he disappears again. This is absolutely crucial now. Do any of you have any questions?"

A combined no was his answer.

"Ok, then get to it. I'll also be sending Forrest and Tanya your way as soon as possible. Forrest has the DHS at his disposal and Tanya will be handling the public information aspect of this work. I will inform the President of the whole situation as we know it now. Be thorough but work as fast of possible. These people have a system to disappear overnight and we can't afford to have that happen. I hope we are not already too late given that several days have passed. Let me know daily of your progress. May God be with you."

While the others prepared to travel, Christian and I began the tedious task of checking whatever paper work they could find on the interlopers. They checked the bank, unfortunately finding all the social security numbers given for the people coming into the area were bogus, either stolen or those of dead people. At the school a similar story emerged leaving them with no possible identity information to follow up on. These people were like ghosts, another similarity to the aftermath of 10/10.

CHAPTER 24

Let's Catch an Agent: Pasadena, TX

Forrest and Tanya were the last to arrive and we gathered to plot our next move. We prayed for guidance and divine intervention on our behalf before beginning the investigation. We knew our time was short; the enemy never wasted time moving their people once a mission was complete

After a short discussion, we decided that staking out the closest Mosque, located near Bycycle would be our best chance of finding our ghost. I gave the order to have two team members with different vehicles watch the Mosque, rotating the members covering the mosque 24/7. "We do not want members of the Mosque to spot us making the chase harder. I'll coordinate with the FBI for additional bodies to assist in the stakeouts of the other mosques in the local area. Dan and Bill, you take the first rotation." They left to take position within eye sight of both the front and back of the building.

"Marcus and Jeremy, you begin an 'investigation' with the businesses and residents in and around the Mosque to see if anyone recognizes Charles' picture. Tell them he has information on possible suspects in the oil refinery attacks.

It will be time consuming and less than likely to gather any real information but it has to be done."

"Tanya and I, will act as a couple, hopefully appearing less threatening in order to question the people in the area, they are mostly elderly couples or lonely widows." This statement raised a few eyebrows and a few chuckles. I blushed, creating laughter among the team.

"Christian and Forrest, I want you working with the local police and FBI to check out any clues coming into those offices. Forrest's position with DHS will give us quick access without involving the President or his Chief of Staff. The local authorities are under a great deal of pressure to find out how this attack happened right under their noses and they want our help.

Nothing happened for day and a half. We continued the surveillance and were trying to remain patient but the constant media coverage kept us on edge. This was the most important thing we could be doing but just watching and asking questions was a bit wearing, but it did pay off finally.

Christian and Forrest interviewed a drug store owner two doors down from the first Mosque on our list, who remembered seeing both Charles and a group of men he did not recognize come to the Friday prayers the Friday before the 'awful attacks on the refineries'. He had seen Charles the night before and he seemed to be packing his car, a brand-new Buick, black and low to the road. The owner stated, "I was taking out the trash when I saw him. He pointed to it currently sitting in the Mosque parking lot. It was still daylight but nearing dusk. I saw the man clearly and recognized him because he had shopped several times in my store. I sincerely hope this is helpful to you."

Christian and Forrest, elated to have a clue, quickly notified us and Earnest. We called in Bill and Dan as backup and began a careful watch of the Mosque. We want to be there the moment our ghost tried to leave. Our plan was to follow him away from the Mosque until he was alone before arresting him. We do not want anyone from the Mosque interfering with our arrest and just as importantly we don't want them to even be aware of it. Hopefully, this would be the best-case scenario.

It was almost anticlimactic when we finally saw our target saunter out of the Mosque and get in his car. It was late evening and all was quiet around us. No one from the Mosque had accompanied him out. We all tensed as he pulled away, going west. Dan and Bill followed closer since they had been at the front of the building as our man left from the rear of the building.

Christian and Forrest picked up the chase about three miles down the road as the other two turned to run along a parallel road. The two teams alternated following our suspect several times and then Tanya and I arrived to take a turn following him. When our target turned toward the entrance of I-20 going west through a residential area, we decided to make our move. The three cars moved into position, following the input of the local police briefed on their locations, who in turn, advised them on the best possibility of boxing the car in. One came toward the front of their target vehicle, one pulled in behind it, and the third car circled down a side street that ended on the street it was on, blocking any chance of the driver escaping.

Our ghost seemed to be taken by surprise by the emergence of cars blocking every roadway around him. He didn't seem hostile, only surprised. As Forrest approached the vehicle, there was only a question in Charles' mind. *What had he done and who were these people? None appeared to be policemen so he waited quietly, after reaching into the glove compartment grabbing his papers.*

Forrest showed him his badge saying, Sir please exit the vehicle. The suspect replied, Can I asked why you are pulling me ov . Forrest cut him off, "Get out of the car and keep your hands in my sight." The suspect complied and stood quiet, assured that this was some terrible misunderstanding.

Christian joined Forrest and took the suspect into custody without incident. I looked at Dan and said, "Drive his car back to headquarters. The whole thing took place without any unwanted attention. Our suspect just disappeared and no one was the wiser, especially his handlers.

The elated team began the drive back to the Houston DHS headquarters, our suspect dejectedly sitting in the back seat of Christian and Forrest's car, his hands in cuffs. *Why have I been taken into custody. My papers are all in order and no one knows my real identity except my handlers. They took my phone and I had no other way to contact my people and certainly wouldn't under the circumstances. I will not talk and they would eventually have to let me go. They have no proof that I was anything other than what my papers indicated. I have covered my trail completely; they cannot know who I am or had been.*

I made the call to Earnest as soon as we were on the road. I gave the details of the arrest as simply as possible and hung up. As we began the drive back to our headquarters, Tanya's presence in the car made it hard for me to stay focused now that the arrest was over. The excitement of the chase and arrest had kept me focused until now. But now, my awareness threatened to overwhelm me because this woman had haunted my dreams since our meeting with her after the October attacks. I just wasn't sure what I could or would do now.

Earnest was overjoyed with my recount of finding and takedown of our target. He was jubilant and gave a quiet praise to his Lord. He hastened to find the President to give him the news. Finding this needle in a haystack so quickly was a blessing indeed. He hoped that his son-in-law would see it that way. He knew that there were still many questions in David's mind about the Lord. Earnest hoped that soon he and his wife, Earnest's daughter, would see the light.

CHAPTER 25

Breaking the Tension

Tanya and I started the return ride and you could cut the tension between us with a knife. Neither of us said anything for almost ten minutes but suddenly both said, "...what do we do about..." then we both laughed nervously. I cleared my throat and asked, "How have you been?" immediately chastising myself for such a stupid question. I knew she had been all over the news and commentary shows, trying to explain the administration's plans. I also knew it was painfully difficult because the team's very existence was not generally known outside of a few high-level officials. I figured she had the hardest job of us all.

Tanya sat quiet for a while, and then asked, "Have you been to many of the attack sites since 10/10?"

Feeling comfortable with this question, I replied, "Oh, yes, Christian and I have been to all but two, we went to the attack on Black Friday in Atlanta the day of the attack there. It was a mess, lots of people hurt with few clues. We worked on the truck, the roadway, and sought out several undercover guys to no avail. No one seemed able to pinpoint the source of the attack and no one so far has taken credit for it. We know for sure that there are two training camps in Georgia but couldn't find a connection. It is frustrating how clever these people are, they are present, and then they are not. We got extremely lucky to catch our realtor. One person remembering him was our break. We know he is not a perpetrator but he is most definitely a facilitator. Christian and I found his picture in Iowa, again by chance."

Tanya sat still for a moment and then commented, "Don't you think we had help from the Lord? I mean all these 'coincidences' don't just happen; do you think?" Her heart was disturbed because she found this man extremely attractive but she would never marry anyone who wasn't a Christian. Realizing what she was thinking, her thoughts turned to the real questions; "am I really that interested in him, am I jumping to conclusions?"

My heart sank; another believer, I had dreamed about her for so long. Why was everyone put in my path a believer? I sighed deeply. "Tanya, I just don't know anything about that for sure. I am sorry to say that I used to go to church with my wife but I was never into it as you and the rest of the team seem to be. When my wife died in a car accident while I was in Iraq, and I... I lost any concept of a loving Lord. She loved the Lord with all her heart and He just took her, so young and full of life. The guys have talked and talked to me and they've been great not to push. But I have a hard time reconciling what they say with what happened. I loved my wife, envisioned a long life, and someday children to the point it hurts when we get together as a group, you know, cook outs, that sort of things. I see my friends so happy, their children so great, and I miss having a chance at that. I feel the Lord deprived me of that joy. My feelings are so mixed up. I have struggled with relationships because of my dread of losing the love for my wife? What do I do with all these mixed-up feelings?" All this poured out of me like water breaking through a dam suddenly. I hadn't expected to say any of this to her but being alone with her in a car while we were following a terrorist made me grow to admire her even more. So, with the tension of the chase over, and with her comment, all the mixed-up feelings just broke loose. I stared straight ahead, waiting for her to laugh or be angry, ashamed of my loss of control.

Tanya again sat quiet for a moment taking in all he had poured out, a sinking feeling when he said he had a wife, then a great sorrow for his loss. She gently reached over to touch his hand so tightly gripping the steering wheel. "Oh, John, what a burden you have been carrying. I am so sorry for your loss. I can understand your fear, but love never truly dies, the more you give, the more you receive. I believe you can maintain that love and give more love to another. You don't stop loving one child when you have another, your love just grows."

I felt a tingle run up my arm when she touched my hand. I felt awkward like I had felt when I first met my wife and now, again upon our first intimate conversation as well. I was stumbling to try to find something else to say, and she could feel the awkwardness of the situation. She said; "I'm sorry," as she drew her hand back, "I didn't mean to bother you." Blushing, I quickly said, "No you are fine, I am just finding it hard to concentrate." She laughed saying, "So am I." I felt myself jerk when I heard that, I had never dreamed she might have felt something too. She again touched my hand.

"I think I will pray for you to trust and have peace for just a while as we sort this out. We will just have to trust God with this whole situation, maybe He can relieve your apprehensions about His love for you. I still trust Him even though I still have nightmares."

"You're suffering from nightmares; I didn't know that." I felt terrible knowing she had been through a terrible experience and now suffered with PTSD. I thought only combat veterans suffered that way but it suddenly occurred to him that that was exactly what she had gone through, a combat situation.

She smiled at his comments and could almost read his thoughts. "Yes, I have nightmares and unexpected loud noises make me jump. But that is not what I think we need to talk about right now. My fondness has grown for you and I have gained a great deal of respect for who you are as a man as I have come to know you in our meetings, rare as they have been. I can feel the tension between us even now. I am not sure where this is going, but perhaps the Lord has something special in mind for us and I personally would like to explore that possibility? Would you?"

I almost bit my tongue. "Yes, yes I would. But you are in Washington and I am in Alabama except when Christian and I are on the road. I think it could be difficult to explore anything this important over that kind of distance."

Tanya smiled that gorgeous smile that I was beginning to adore. "How about we email for a while and plan to go out together, alone, when we do get together in Washington. I don't think the others will notice."

"Ha" I said, "Christian said something the same night we first saw each other. We'll be teased a bit but it will be good natured. I can stand it if you can."

"Good friends are a blessing and I can handle it. I'll write down my email address and you can give me yours. We will all probably go back to our respective places in the next few days. I am game to try going out if we have a chance. I've never been to Houston before."

Grinning, "Sure thing, I have only flown through but I think Dan was stationed at Fort Hood for a while, he might have some suggestions. The hotel might be able to suggest something as well. I think we have a deal!"

She leaned over and patted my hand as we arrived at headquarters and got out. I was thanking my lucky stars. Being put into a tense situation with only one another had allowed us the freedom to start a possible relationship that might lead……anywhere.

We managed one outing for dinner in the two days we remained in Houston. I asked Dan about a good place to eat in the area and he had suggested a steak house and a Mexican restaurant near our hotel. We both offered the excuse of wanting a bit of fresh air and left at different times. We met just outside of the bright lights of the hotel and walked to and dined at the Mexican place he'd suggested.

CHAPTER 26

Facing the Teasing Storm

Two days later as Christian and I boarded the plane returning to Huntsville, Alabama; Christian asked with a smirk, "Well, how did your date with Tanya go?"

I tried to scowl, then with a smothered laugh when I answered, "So how do you figure we had a date?"

Christian laughed out loud! "Brother, we all figured it out over the weeks of meetings in D.C. You two were so determined to ignore each other but the vibes were so strong the rest of us felt it too. We 'arranged' your ride together in Houston with each other just to put all of us out of our misery. You two were so into each other but trying so hard to mask it that we decided to do a little tactical push. And when you both left at different times for 'personal stuff' we all had a good laugh along with high fives all around!"

I must have looked completely chagrined by what my friend was telling me. Tanya and I had thought we had been so 'cool' in sneaking out for our first and only 'date'. To find the team had conspired to throw them together on the hunt for their terrorist was humiliating in a fun sort of way. "We thought we were being brilliantly covert and playing it so close to the chest. I told her we would get some teasing but you guys really pulled a slicky!" I said shaking my head. "But I really appreciate the push; I still don't know where it's going but we are going to stay in touch by email and I guess we don't have to pretend we are doing anything other than seeing where this goes if everyone knows."

Christian just said, "No, we are thrilled for you and she is a great lady that I think just may get you out of that solitary confinement you have locked yourself in. We just couldn't watch two special people who are so attracted to each other creating tension in every meeting we have had. I think Earnest even suspects. I am so glad you have finally given in to the inevitable. You know that Eve and I went through a similar phase; we fought continuously when we first met. It was my mom who laughed and told me that we would have beautiful children! I couldn't believe my ears but here we are and it is so great. I pray the same for you, friend."

I smiled but said, "There is one huge problem, she is a believer like the rest of you and I am still struggling with the whole 'God' thing. She was really sweet about it, saying I could just trust and she would pray. I suspect she will never marry someone who doesn't share her faith. I really don't know what to do about it. I still feel God short-changed me when my wife died in such a stupid accident. How do you deal with those feelings?"

Christian remained quiet so long that I thought maybe he hadn't heard him. But finally, Christian said in a quiet voice, "John, we will never completely understand all of what happens to us in this life. Your wife seemed to really love the Lord and you looked pretty good at it also. But we can't know the whys sometimes. Do you think your wife would have wanted to stay on earth when she could be with her Lord all the time, despite her love for you and for your plans? Would you have kept her from the wonderfulness of being with Jesus if you could have? This is the biggest issue most people have with the Lord. Trust, just everyday trust is the key in hard situations. Trust is tough to capture for most people. I've had my own moments of struggle but I finally resolved it by deciding, just deciding that I either did trust or I did not. A blow like you took, the loss of your wife, is hard, never ever would any of us say it wasn't, but now God has introduced you to someone that just might be the soul mate you long for. Try taking a step back and see if He will show you more of the big picture. He is faithful in all things and you have been running from Him for a long time. Stop and let Him comfort your heart, mind, and soul. I want you to think about that and then let's talk again."

I simply nodded my head, my mind and heart too full of maybes that I couldn't say anything. I trust Christian like the brother I never had and appreciated what he was saying. I thought that I would think, and maybe even pray and see what happened.

CHAPTER 27

The Mental Chess Game

Two weeks later Tumbrel/Charles still sat quietly in the holding area of DHS's D.C. headquarters. *I haven't said anything, but I'm worrying in silence what 'The Ghost' was thinking. I knew that for all intents and purposes, I disappeared without a trace. They even had my phone and still had not tried to interrogate me. I thought that saying nothing at all would force them to release me after a few days. I was not asked and did not volunteer any information but only answered as Charles Arndell. My mind mulling over how I was caught.*

I'm stuck in a blank holding room considering my options. There didn't really seem to be many because I still didn't know why they had arrested me or why I was being held. It had been a week and a half since those men arrested me on my way out of Houston and no one seemed to have the least interest in me. It was so strange; my mind ran constantly as I kept going over and over what had happened. Even in my sleep, I dreamed of the past two years of my life, the work I had accomplished for Allah. But I never got to a place of resolution for my dilemma.

During the night, my restless mind continued its feverish search for answers causing me to dream, so vividly, about my entrance into this country on that warm July 4th.

I could feel the rocking of the fishing boat *as I arrived, standing in excitement and awe that I had so easily entered this country, my only goal for the last four years. I still remembered the meeting in the Chechen Republic that had seared my soul and brought me to this place and time. I had often thought of the quiet man who spoke so movingly about the cause for Allah and the spreading of our faith, and taking the fight to the infidels, a major thrust of Islam. I remembered how my heart caught fire at the thought of moving to the belly of the Great Satan and making them pay for their many sins, like their decadent living but mostly for not being Muslim.*

I recalled my mother's sobbing giving me a momentary pause, but she quickly told me; "These are tears of joy, my son, I am so proud that you are following our faith and will have a chance to allow Allah to use you in the coming mission. "I came from a poor home in Chechnya, growing up in the midst of changing governments in my country. He wanted to help al Qaeda, whose mission I didn't think I would ever have a chance to help, but Allah had provided an opportunity beyond my dreams. I was going to help a group that I greatly admired.

Al Qaeda sent me to England to perfect my grasp of English and to learn western ways. When my training there finally complete, I was sent to Canada in order to facilitate my move to the United States.

I was picked up once I cleared Canadian customs and was driven through Canada during the night with nothing of import being said. I remembered being tired and hungry, but this was a small sacrifice to make for Allah. I boarded a dirty smelly fishing boat on a rotting pier on the Canadian coast of Lake Superior. I spent most of the night throwing up as the boat rolled constantly. This was my first ride on a boat in such a large body of water and the stench and motion made me sick even as they untied from the pier. My arrival in Duluth, Minnesota on a holiday in a fishing boat had assured my easy entry since the local harbor personnel were dealing with an over flowing bay filled with small craft and Americans eating and drinking to excess. The local authorities were too busy to ask questions. The group's support cell provided me the proper paper work, showing I had always been a 'citizen' of the United States. I was glad to be off the boat and anyone seeing me, would think I was just another drunk partier getting off a boat. Once my stomach settled I grew excited to begin the quest for which Allah had prepared me.

I felt out of place, knowing someone was supposed to meet me, but I didn't have a clue as to who or how. I considered my situation, so as to not make myself stand out; I started looking around with at least an appearance of interest. I wondered how long it would be before someone would contact me and take me to the place, I had been sent across the world to help build. I was so wound up that I had trouble remembering the English that I'd been so carefully taught. I laughed to myself because even though I spoke English with some fluency, I was having trouble understanding the strange dialect I was hearing. I knew they were speaking English, but it sounded so different than the British version of English. Having no further instructions to follow, I leaned up against a pylon on the pier and waited for my guide in this new and strange place.

I was unaware that at the moment, that someone was carefully observing me as I waited. Martin Wraith, who turned out to be my local contact, told me later, he was laughing at me, noting my somewhat green appearance and the obvious disheveled appearance of someone finishing a long trip. He had seen this look before, but he noticed that I looked comfortable in my jeans and t-shirt. I looked like I belonged, even down to looking like I had a hangover.

Martin Wraith later told me how pleased he had been when he first saw me. "Your handlers knew your background, but said you are perfect for this mission because your hair is kind of medium blonde, your slight build, and you are about 5 feet 10 inches tall. You also have gray eyes under straight eyebrows." l learned later that Martin had come from the United Arab Emirates and had been in the U.S. for about eight years. Martin actually enjoyed his life except for the cold winters of Minnesota. His only complaint was why the powers that be had picked a place so cold for people who were from the warm areas of the Middle East. Many guessed at the reasons, but no one really knew, because all of Allah's soldiers knew not ask questions.'

Martin finally approached me, saying, "Timothy" in English, the English of the "colonies", a phrase that had always amused Martin.

"Welcome, 'cousin'. I know you are tired and hungry. Grab your backpack and let's go home." After a slight hesitation, I responded in passable English. "Oh, I am starved and ready for a long nap. I hope your house is not far." Martin looked like someone he would know. Stout, about 5 feet, 9 inches, dark bushy hair with touches of gray, a dark mustache, and a dark complexion, he could have been any of my uncles. Only I and from what I had heard, a cousin had inherited the light hair and complexion of a

great, great grandmother from England. This had been the bane of my existence as a child and youth. Teased, ridiculed, and taunted for being different, I had sworn to myself that when I could, I would change my appearance. Now it was clear that Allah had arranged all this across time and cultures.

Because of the rift in the family over my father decision to abandon the Russian Orthodox Christian faith for Islam, there had been little or no communication between the families. Thus, I did not know if the cousin was male or female or what that person had gone through as a result of their looks. And I didn't much care, they were Infidels to me.

The two of us moved to a car in the parking area and soon Martin had worked his way out of the dock area. Driving through Duluth proper and onto the south-bound entrance to I-35 they began the drive back to my new 'home'.

With the blue skies and the warm temperatures, Martin drove with the windows down and the smell of many barbecues' grills wafted into the car, causing both men's stomachs to rumble. "We should be home soon," Martin reassured me. In the end, the trip took a bit over an hour, and because of the holiday, traffic was quiet according to Martin. I could not imagine more traffic.

"My wife will have a nice dinner ready and your room prepared." I just nodded. I wasn't positive just what all Martin had said and didn't want to look a fool. I figured that I would understand when we got there.

I remembered being overwhelmed by the large expanse, the number of buildings, industrial areas, and parks I saw as we drove down I-35. "Maybe I am just tired from all the travel," I thought. "I was a little afraid of the burly man who had met me but right now, they could kill me and send me on to paradise." I was hungry, tired, wanted a decent meal, not fries and a hamburger, and then to just a chance to lay down.

Martin finally pulled off the interstate at the second Minneapolis exit and smoothly transitioned to the city traffic, again light because of the holiday. Seven blocks later he turned into a quiet suburban street and reached his home. He looked at it with a touch of pride. It didn't really belong to him, the money had come from the cause, but Martin was proud of the care he had showered on the landscaping and keeping the house in tiptop shape. It glowed with the evening lights. He sighed with satisfaction. He had a nice home, a good wife, three children, and a cause to help. It was Allah's gift to a good Muslim, all and more than he could hope for; except paradise of course. Soon, Allah, soon; he murmured.

I stared at Martin's house, a large two-story colonial, with white vinyl siding and dark red shutters. These were details I knew nothing about, like colonial style and vinyl siding, but would quickly learn. It had a large lawn area and flowers planted about in a most pleasant way. I had never seen a house this big for one family, why one could almost play a game of soccer on the yard! Grabbing my dark green backpack, I walked up a straight paved walk and entered the house and felt I had entered a rich person's house. A spacious living room, dining room combination stretched out before me. It seemed a calm place with small touches of a red color, a large couch, several large chairs, tables, and a piano in the corner. Martin called me and I followed his voice into the kitchen. I stood for a moment and wondered about a people who lived in such splendor. Not one of my family, friends, or to my knowledge had ever lived like this.

Martin showed me to the small half bath off the kitchen and said, "Wash up for supper in here." I was overcome with the splendor of it all. Martin finally introduced me to Marta, his wife, I quickly noticed that she seemed to feel free to comment on the day's events, even asking me if I'd had a good trip. I didn't understand this freedom and for now I was too tired to care. After eating a hardy meal, Martin seeing my exhaustion, led me up the stairs and toward a room at the end of a long hallway.

I gladly closed the door after Martin's simple good night and stood looking at my assigned room. It was bigger than any space I had ever lived in. I could have had four or five others in this size of space back home. Even during my stay in England, many 'students' had stayed in smaller houses, many to a room. My travel through Canada had been so rapid that I had only slept in a moving vehicle, using the facilities at gas stations along the way.

I had slowly managed to stop thinking as a Muslim in public. We had been warned to be very careful about this among the infidels we'd associate with. I never learned to like the name they had given me, Timothy Arrow, It was ugly name, but those who trained me had never let me answer to anything else. I doubted I would ever like the new name but I practiced it by saying it out loud and having my brothers at the Mosque call me it over and over so that my reaction would become natural.

My stay with this family took only long enough for me to get situated and for the local mosque to get me some training with a local realtor who was a member of the mosque. When I was deemed ready, I was told to move to Iowa, a State I had to look up on the internet and wondered at the choice. "But it is for Allah and to Iowa I will go." Arriving in Fort Dodge, I went first to my local contact who said, "The first order of business is to get you established with a local realtor. Then you will find a suitable place to establish a training camp for Allah's soldiers."

I found a place just outside Fort Dodge, a state park with the only woods I could find in the area. The land was flat and mostly farming fields. I had never in my life seen so much open land. Everything about this place was beyond the imagination of a person who had grown up in a mountainous and rugged place like Chechnya. It was only the continual fighting that I didn't miss.

I soon was able to establish myself as a realtor in a small office in Ames and began the process of buying up land with homes for my 'customers'. The people were arriving in small groups and began building in that small area around their houses a tight but satisfactory training compound.

CHAPTER 28

Questioning the Past?

That morning, in my confined area, my mind forced me to continue considering each step of my life in the U.S. I was looking for the mistake, the one mistake that had brought me to this unknown prison. Both in Iowa and Texas, "Nothing flashy or attention getting." But here I am in this room not knowing what tomorrow might bring despite the careful planning and execution of that plan. "Just where did I go wrong?"

I remembered the night that Fletcher Cordell, "My inspiration", had visited me. Stunned to even see the man again, I listened; "You will go to Houston, Texas by the weekend." With shame I remembered that I had started to argue with the man. Fletcher had rebuked me quickly; "don't get into the habit of thinking too much like our enemy, leave no trace for the enemy to find. Get rid of everything and wash everything down so that not even a fingerprint or DNA sample can be found. This will lead the investigators to a dead end." All his other instructions had been about how to dispose of my things.

I had been rejoicing in my apartment about the wonderful attacks that had sent the nation into frenzy and Fletcher had smiled in agreement but again urged my departure. "Four attacks in one day, all at virtually the same time! It is wonderful, but now you are to leave this place and go to Houston.

Fletcher said, "Goodbye and, "Assalamu 'Alaikum".

"Wa'alaikum Assalam" I answered. After a handshake, both went to the door and Fletcher disappeared into the night. I knew his reputation, 'the Ghost.'

"All I know about Houston was the team, the Houston Texans!" I thought, "Another new name," and how will I find a place there? But again, Allah would provide. I understood and would work to make it real in my heart, as I had with my first new name.

I soon realized that cleaning the office must be done now, in the dark so no one would question what I was doing. I grabbed my coat and raced down to the office.

After reaching the realtor's office, I entered without turning on any lights. I didn't want to create suspicion that I was ever there, even the chance of a passerby noting lights at such an odd hour. I turned on the flashlight to see just what I was doing. And realized I would have to wipe down everything to ensure there wouldn't be any fingerprints, or DNA, during an investigation of my disappearance. I was sure my boss would start a missing person investigation. After all, I had been very successful for the office.

Going quickly through my desk, removing all traces of my existence; papers, upcoming deals, notes, all of it found its way into a trash bag. I opened the janitor's closet, took out cleanser and rags, and began a thorough cleaning of the desk, the coffee area, the bathrooms, and even the other desks and front counter. My eye hit upon the pictured array of realtors on the wall and I cursed myself for forgetting that detail. I carefully removed the pictures, and scrubbed the whole wall to remove any faint outline where another picture had hung, then hung the other pictures back on the wall. I searched the file cabinets for any reference to myself, frustrated to find the owner's file cabinet locked but confident that she did not keep anything about me in it. Finally, in the wee hours of the night, feeling that I was finished, I took one last look around the office to assure myself that I had left nothing to chance; I walked out and headed home.

The next day I began the same cleansing process for my apartment to ensure no one would ever find anything to connect the place with me. I was thankful it was a weekend and it would just look like I was doing some chores around the house. I carefully washed everything down with Clorox including the walls, all the furniture, anything permanently a part of the rooms. I took all the linens, towels, curtains, and toiletries and put them in another trash bag. Considering all I had done, going over each step in my mind, assured that I had accomplished all the assigned tasks, I loaded all the garbage bags into my car. My next feat would be disappearing. The whole idea of disappearing without a trace tickled me.

As I waited for nightfall to leave, I thought of my work, knowing that I had served Allah with all my heart and could hear and see the results in the conversations of the people around me. It was exhilarating. Per my training, I dumped one of the garbage bags in a dumpster behind a restaurant several towns later. The rest would end up scattered in different towns across my travels, making it less likely anyone would tie the location to me and the rotting food really messed up the papers and linens.

My thoughts were interrupted by the guard bringing in my supper and I felt the anger grow inside me. I would like to knock that guy out and run for it, but I feared without knowing anything about my location, that it would be a futile short attempt. I couldn't make a foolish move but I would soon have to make some kind of move, but just what that move would be was beyond me. I had no access to other people like I had thought I would and no way to get somewhere if I did 'break out' so I pondered as I ate the meal. It was soon going to be time to demand 'something'. My thoughts turned again to my past, perhaps hoping that the stirring of my memories would tell the tale of how I had been caught.

After a long previous night and another long drive through the night, I arrived in Kansas City and, using the GPS device in my car, drove straight to the Mosque located in the city. I had dropped the apartment keys in the dumpster at a 7-11 after I had dumped the garbage bags in several previous towns; there would be little left that could associate me with Timothy Arrow.

Arriving in the late evening, I was greeted by one of the men who lived onsite. At the mention of my original name, I was taken straight to their Imam. He greeted me warmly and told me, I was expected. I was assured that all was in order and we would discuss our business in the morning. I was shown to a room where I could spend the night.

I was relieved to be able to sleep and gather my thoughts. While I was tired, it had also been a period of high adrenalin and now, I crashed physically, but my mind would not quiet down. It took a while for my thoughts to slow and for exhaustion to finally push me into a deep sleep.

It took a week for my appearance to change. My hair grew out and I dyed it a soft brown and donned fake glasses. This allowed them to finish my new identity and for the Mosque to coordinate for me to buy another car at a local dealership.

Finally, I prepared to depart after the Imam blessed me and my endeavors. As I left the building, I sighed as I took my few possessions and walked to the local car dealer. The Mosque was centrally located in the city near a number of businesses and the walk was an easy one.

I thought about the car, I liked flashy cars, but knew that it would not fit my new persona. I finally chose a black Audi A5 Sportback but included all the 'bells and whistles' for myself. The dealer was a bit surprised that I paid in cash but I told him a fanciful story about a great uncle dying and leaving me a 'wad' of money and that I wanted the thrill of owning a brand-new car without any payments. The dealer smiled at the enthusiasm of a young man, handed me the keys, shook my hand and said "Good Luck, Charles."

Laughing to myself, I rejoiced again that my looks allowed me to blend in without any problems. I now understood fully why Allah had blessed me with an appearance that would allow me to fulfill my mission with less trouble.

With my newly minted name, "Charles Arndell," I took the Interstate leading to Texas and began my newest journey in this land that fascinated and repelled my Muslim sensitivities. Using the new name and credit card at a motel just off the interstate in Dallas, still sounded strange but I would persist. I'd learned to respond to Timothy Arrow and it had become second nature to me. I would learn to respond to this new name with just a little time. In the meantime, I would have to stay alert and on guard.

Arriving in Houston, I was exhausted, so I stayed in a hotel just north of the Houston Mosque. It was also too late to contact anyone at the mosque. It also felt good to have arrived at my destination. I had the name and address of the Mosque so I could show up for Friday Prayers. I bowed my head thanking Allah for blessing this trip.

After a night's rest, I drove straight to the Mosque and approached the Imam. I was expected and taken to an apartment on the premises and settled in. After a brief discussion of my need for a few clothes and other necessities, the Imam left to make arrangements to obtain the required items.

CHAPTER 29

The Breaking Point

Now, after two weeks of no interrogation or conversation, I decided to ramp up the situation by demanding a lawyer even at this late date, the laws of this country should still be in effect, I would use their antiquated constitution against them. My people often used the laws of this nation and others against them to our benefit.

So, when the guard brought my lunch, I said, "I want to speak with a lawyer and bring this farce to an end." The guard only nodded, turned, and left the room. I was surprised that my demand hadn't flustered the guard, not even a slight flinch in his demeanor. Just what did that mean?

Several hours later, I found out. Two burly men entered and escorted me to a smaller room without windows that I recognized as an interrogation room. I didn't understand, didn't these people know I was an American citizen with the rights and privileges of one? Then a man with vaguely familiar face entered the room with a handful of papers in his hand.

"Good evening, sir," the guard said, "can I have your name?" I pulled my ID and said, "John Banks, from Huntsville, Alabama." I had just come in from Huntsville after getting a call that the prisoner has demanded a lawyer.

I was let in and looked in on our guest. Looking straight at our guest seated at the table, I agreed that he certainly didn't look like a foreigner. With his blond/brown hair, blue eyes, and very fair skin he could have passed as anyone from a western culture. I was still confused that Jews are considered oriental based on the teachings of a Messianic Jew that Christian had shared with the team a few months back. But that was really immaterial at the moment.

I studied what little we actually knew about this man and it was confusing. His paperwork looked perfect, almost too perfect. His fingerprints were only on file as Timothy Arrow in Iowa and Charles Arndell in Texas. If he had not been caught in the aftermath of the plane crashes into four of the largest refineries in Texas, no one would ever have discovered the duplication because the FBI Fingerprint Data Center had a backlog of requests from law enforcement agencies requesting fingerprints related to criminal activity and the terrorist attacks from 10/10.

We, the team knew "Timothy" was instrumental in getting terrorists into the town of Bycycle, and facilitating the buying of properties in the area. Plus, the report from the Iowan Realtor who told them that he was indeed the realtor for buying the properties used by the terrorists involved in the 10/10 attacks last fall. There, he had also shown up at her door with a charming manner and apparently endless access to lots of money.

So, where had he really come from, what was his source, and how did he get into the country? We had not found a birth certificate for either name anywhere in the country. He had just appeared. Now, my team and I had the job of trying to break his silence to learn something, anything.

I slapped the papers down on the table, startling this man of great restraint. Charles looked up at me and I could see his resolve that he would not speak to me. Although I towered over him and watched him, Timothy didn't appear phased because we later learned he had been brought up by some of the toughest fighters in Chechnya. He felt he could hold his own, after all, we knew nothing at all about him.

I watched as no emotion floated across the man's face, knowing he felt safe in not talking. I had discussed this moment with the team almost every day waiting for his first move. We had just enough information about him to hold him but not enough to break him. We had to figure out just what motivated him and use his weakest point to get to him. We had been waiting for him to ask for a lawyer and been somewhat surprised that in the end, it took two long weeks for him to play this card. We had him dead to rights as a terrorist but he didn't know that yet. So, we could hold him without a lawyer under the Patriot Act as a terrorist. We knew, of course, that eventually he would have a lawyer but for now, no one but the ten people involved with the President's Team and the head of Homeland Security knew who or where he was. The guards only knew that he was an important suspect but not what he was being held for.

The final decision came from Earnest Trowbridge after some consultation from an FBI interrogation specialist. Call him by the Iowa name and see what happens. It was just that simple in this game of cat and mouse except the mouse was not aware of all the cat knew.

I was chosen to talk with him because I knew the Iowa area better than anyone else on the team. I had been the one to discover the presence of a terrorist camp in Iowa while visiting my late wife's parents.

I sat down at the table and said quietly, "Afraid not, Timothy." I watched as the man jerked slightly, so slightly that if I had not been watching for it, I might have missed it.

"I have no idea what you are talking about, my name is Charles Arndell and I am a citizen of Texas, a realtor in good standing. I demand to see a lawyer." He had an irate look on his face.

I smiled, "Afraid not Timothy Arrow. You see we know about your 'real estate' activities in Texas and also in Iowa." I pulled out the picture from the Iowa Realty Office the owner had in her locked file and slid it across the table at him. "So, you are here in our custody as a terrorist under the Patriot Act. We know that you 'bought the land and houses for the terrorists who carried out the attacks of Oct 10th last year and also the houses, and business in Texas for the attacks on the oil refineries. So, you will go to prison for the rest of your life, possibly at Fort Leavenworth or at Guantanamo Bay, makes no difference to me which it is. We have your picture from Iowa and the statement of the realtor you bamboozled in Texas. You are responsible for a lot of hurt and death in both places and we don't care where you end up but you won't die a 'martyr's death'."

Timothy/Charles' countenance took on a look of completely stunned amazement. "No you can't," was all he could say. I could see his mind whirling.

Timothy's mind was scrambling, it couldn't be, I'd been so careful, cleaned everything out, removing my DNA and fingerprints. They could not, no, no, no, did that realtor in Iowa have that picture in that stupid locked file drawer? Oh, Allah, how could I have been so brainless? But after the shower of emotions, I locked myself back into the prison of silence. I glared at my accuser, but had no other comments to make. I will just stay silent and still and they can't or wouldn't get anything from me. That was the mission's core rule; never ever talk to the enemy.

I had hoped that my 'credentials' as an American citizen would shield me from any treatment under the Patriot Act and I could use my 'citizenship' as a way to avoid or prolong any questioning these infidels might try on me. But now, that was blown away by a stupid picture and a lady with an intense need to protect her client's privacy, thus the locked file cabinet. Strange how the simplest of habits can be our undoing, whether ours or someone we work with. I would have to ponder that a while. But I would not say another word even if they water boarded me, no I wouldn't.

I left the room with a small sense of triumph but it was sure smaller than I'd hoped for. I gathered with the team members and tried to plot a way forward. But how do you make someone talk if they did not want to talk? I personally thought I would not hesitate to 'torture' anyone who had caused harm to my country and its people if it helps saved lives. But I also knew that my fellow team members would not nor would Earnest condone that. If I thought about it long enough, neither would I but my anger and desire to punish someone was very strong right then. And I appreciated that I had so many mentors who could keep me straight in my thinking.

Our problem was stuck in all our minds almost to the exclusion of all else. What could we do to get this person to talk? Would it be truthful or more lies in the end, if he did talk? The problem so many have in the military is that having been asked to do the unthinkable, they are then asked to be 'normal' human beings; whatever 'normal' meant when they came home. The military had been railed against for shooting dead people in Iraqi homes but the sad reality was that some of them 'played dead' and then rose up to kill soldiers moving through the house to clear it. There seemed to be no clear line of what was acceptable and what was not for the people who put it all on the line for the nation.

Other experiences in the theater of the 'War on Terror' and in Vietnam had taught the soldier valuable lessons in survival in an atmosphere where 'the rules' applied today and maybe didn't the next day. One couldn't shoot into a Mosque even if the gunfire that killed your buddy came from there. One didn't shoot children even if that child was carrying a grenade in its hand to 'give' to you. So, there was almost literality no rules and heaven help you if you were caught breaking one of them.

As I sat in my office, shared by the team and pondered the possibilities of getting this particular terrorist to talk, not knowing his background or anything of import about him made deciding what made him tick difficult. He didn't 'look' like the others the team had run across in following up on the 10/10 attacks, he had no accent to speak of except a slight touch of British. He wasn't in any data base of any kind anywhere in the world. He was truly a ghost except we could see and touch him. I knew the other team members were praying for a breakthrough and I hoped it worked for them. I was personally at my wits end. I was supposed to be in charge of this team but I had no clues of what or where to go next.

In our home away from home, a nice but not flashy hotel near the DHS Headquarters, the others were indeed praying. They offered their questions to the only one they knew of who actually knew who their man was and where he was from. It was a quiet endeavor, none of them wanting their true purposes to be leaked out because someone overheard them talking or even praying. It was evening and they had been at it since early morning. They decided to leave it in the Hands of their Father and go eat somewhere new. I had just arrived looking worn down with responsibilities, so we decided to go to a restaurant one of their contacts at DHS had told them about.

CHAPTER 30

Revealing a Ghost at Dinner

I tried to decline but the team insisted, so I gave up, changed clothes to a more casual look, and went out with them. The place was owned by Chechen expats and was lively and noisy. The music was traditional and it certainly enlivened the men and they sincerely enjoyed the food.

The change came when the evening entertainment began. A lovely young woman came out on the small stage carrying a violin. She began a song full of soul and ethos but it was how she looked that captured the team's interest. She was blonde and very fair singing a Chechen song in the language of Chechnya with a healthy dose of charm. We were disconcerted because of how she looked and that she sang with a husky voice that almost vibrated off the walls. She reminded us of our culprit. Now we knew that a lot of Russians were fair and blonde but this was a Chechen restaurant, a province of the old Soviet Union. Chechens were not necessarily a fair and blonde people. The Chechen history is full of battles over who owned the land, where the original immigrants came from but the main theory is that the settlers moved out of the Fertile Crescent which covers Upper Egypt, Mesopotamia, or the Middle East area known as the cradle of civilization. The music was in line with the home area of the Chechen patrons.

We were the object of some covert looks from the other patrons but no one approached us outside of the waitress. Certainly, there were questions quietly asked by other customers but it was all just questions.

We immediately began to try to figure out how to find out about this young woman. Christian finally came up with an idea. When the waitress approached with our bills, he gently asked about the singer. He said he was taken with the song and would like to know more about it. The waitress smiled and said she would ask the young lady to come over to explain but that the owner would come also since this was the rule. Christian smiled his consent.

As the owner and singer approached, we scooted chairs to make a place for them, standing as the young woman arrived. She smiled at our courtesy. The owner pulled out the chair for her and seated her with a flourish. We all sat and asked our question again, Christian taking the lead. "Can you tell us about that song?" She smiled and speaking in fairly descent English told us the story of a love lost through war, a sentiment we could connect with, expressly me.

With good will abounding, Christian asked the singer, "Where are you from and how did you come to the U.S?" Looking down for a moment, she answered, "I am from the mountains of Chechnya and I was sent by my family to escape the fighting in our nation." Christian murmured, "I am so sorry you are missing home." Moving along he asked, "Can you tell me about your family? You have piqued my interest about life in Chechnya." She replied, "I am the daughter of a village leader and that because of my looks my father sent me to my uncle in the U.S. My father feared that I would be bullied as my cousin had been." A questioning eyebrow was all Christian did. She freely went on to say, "My first cousin, Tumbrel, was severely teased and bullied because he looked like I do as the result of having a distant relative who had been English, quite the lovely English rose from the family tales."

Christian asked in the most sympatric voice he could muster, "What happened to your cousin?" She sighed, "He just disappeared about six years ago and my family has no idea what happened to him."

Christian softly asked, "What was his full name? Maybe we can help your family find him or what happened to him."

"Oh, Tumbrel Pandya. His father was my father's brother but there is little contact between the relatives, since my uncle's family embraced Islam while my father remained loyal to the Russian Orthodox Church. It caused a lot of problems for the whole family and broke my grandmother's heart. But I don't know any more than that. As I said, there is little contact between the families."

We all complimented her on the song and her singing, also complimenting the owner. His only comment during the entire conversation was that he was the singer's uncle and he was pleased to have been able to take care of her and see to her education.

We left a huge tip and strolled out of the restaurant. Outside, far from the possibility of being seen, we shared high fives all around.

Christian said, "Thank you, God." Supported by a few "Amens." from the other team mates. Even I acknowledged that this was nothing short of a miracle. I could see the miracle aspect of this, more clearly than anything since my wife's death.

I called Earnest as we walked back to the hotel. Earnest also gave praise to the Lord as well saying, "Praise God, I will start a thorough search on the name ASAP. It might be a tough find but nothing was impossible with the Lord." During the next two days, a team of analysts combed through both national and international data bases without a single mention of that name. The young woman's name came up as a young child brought in to live with an uncle in this area and the paperwork was all in order. She was in fact, exactly who she had told them she was. This began a cross reference with her family in the Chechen Republic. This would take much longer since it was still in the throes of an internal war.

Back at the hotel, I spoke softly, "Christian, uh," muttering uncomfortably when they returned to their quarters.

"Yeah, John, what is it?" Christian turned away from the door and back to the center of the room where I stood hesitantly.

"Well, uh, I did see the miracle of finding that young lady in such a strange way and, uh, I was wondering what I would have to do, uh, you know." I said not looking up.

"Actually, no I don't know for sure," Christian said with a smile on his face growing.

"Uh, what does one do to be a real Christian? I mean like you guys, and Tanya? Is it hard, you all seem so comfortable talking with and about God and I don't know the first thing about it and..." looking up I stared at Christian. "You aren't going to make this easy, are you?"

"John, I'm not trying to do anything but see how serious you are. You've played a good part before. The hard thing about becoming a Christian is deciding to believe that it is true. Knowing God personally takes spending time with Him, trusting Him, and letting Him lead you. We humans aren't very good at that, especially letting Him lead and I don't want you to make a decision just because it feels good right this minute, OK?"

"Well, I have been thinking about our talk and you saying you struggled some also and tonight, I saw with my own eyes what all of you have been telling me for, I guess, months. I couldn't believe my eyes or brain when I saw that girl and then to learn what we did, it was miraculous, it was! Now I want to be sure that I have that assurance also, to know that I'll see Evelyn again and maybe even have something with Tanya. These thoughts have been circling in my mind over and over and coming to only one conclusion, I need what you have in my life, tonight was just icing on the cake, so to speak."

"Ok, that seems right to me. Here's what we will do if you are ok with it. I'm going to call the others over here and we will all lead you in the prayer." Christian answered. "They have all been praying for you all this time and would like to be a part of it. OK?"

"Uh, ok, I guess. I just didn't expect it to be such a big deal."

"Oh, John, you have no idea how big a deal it is for all of us. This is the second answer to prayer in about two hours on the same day! Hold on just a minute."

About five minutes later, the whole crew banged on the door and as soon as Christian opened it, in unison, "Did you find something else out, you sounded urgent over the phone?"

"No, no, something better than that!" Christian watched the skepticism flow over their faces. "I mean really better; John is asking to receive Jesus as his Savior and I knew you all would want to be part of it."

A firm, "Thank you Lord," passed quickly from the lips of each man. Christian motioned for each to kneel and then each repeated the Sinner's Prayer with me. For two hours they talked about each word, what it meant and each giving me a quick testimony of their experience. Still feeling elated and joyous, they finally left and returned to their rooms. Each of them slept better that night than they had since this whole mess started. Christian made a quiet phone call to the Earnest, the COS and let him know the good news. Earnest laughed and said, "Should I tell the rest of the team?" He was hinting about Tanya. Christian just laughed and said, "I will leave that up to your sage wisdom."

CHAPTER 31

The Next to Last Puzzle, Washington DC

We discussed the new information trying to decide how to best use it. After a lengthy debate, we made a decision.

We waited two days, allowing our suspect to sweat his confession out, I finally entered the room saying, "Good morning Tumbrel Pandya." Everyone else was behind the two-way mirror watching his reaction, which was immediate. He jumped to his feet and shouted, "How?"

We watched as dismay cross his face and he sank down into the seat, his head resting on his chest, eyes closed. We could see his mind racing, as he pondered his situation. He had given himself away and was beginning to fear the worst. During our debate, we surmised that his thoughts would run along the lines of: *If these people didn't kill me, then my masters would.* His fear was justified for giving the enemy information by losing control was tantamount to betrayal in his world. As his mind seem to settle on his situation, his eyes rose to meet mine. I said, "We know who you are, where you come from and about your family. It is time for your breakfast, ponder those things and we'll talk later."

We then let Tumbrel sit in his room for two days. He ate nothing and drank very little water. He was waiting to be marched outside and summarily executed. It would be what happened to anyone in his home country who betrayed the innate principals of the cause.

We went over our next step carefully. We wanted information but sensed that our captive was on the verge of a total breakdown. We wanted to approach him gingerly to get the desired result. Since I had been the one to reveal the fact that we knew his real identity, we decided I would go at the young man again. I prayed almost constantly, preparing myself for this important job. Finally, when I felt ready, I took my notes and entered the cell Tumbrel was in. The cell was less stark than the interrogation room but only by a little.

I entered the room where Tumbrel lay quietly on the cot. Sitting in the only chair, I watched the rise and fall of the man's chest. After about five minutes, Tumbrel opened his eyes and looked at me. He said in a husky voice, "What do you want now?"

I just smiled and answered, "Why, nothing much. We were wondering where you were going when you left the mosque in Houston. That's not too hard to say now, is it?"

Tumbrel sighed, "Not that it matters now, because I am not where I am supposed to be and they will change everything anyway. I was a small cog in a big wheel."

I smiled again, "If you say so, but I would still like to know what you were doing, kind of wraps things up for me."

"I don't think it will but," Tumbrel sighed again. "I got all my orders from the Imams just like everyone and the Imams only know what little they know. The whole system works on the idea that you can't tell what you don't know."

"Do you know who is in charge?" I asked.

"Only one," Tumbrel replied in a low voice, and then he continued. "Only one, the man I heard in Chechnya, a man with a beautiful voice and a scar across half his face. He never really smiles because of it. But I have only seen him three times, first in Chechnya, once in Minneapolis, and once more in Ames when he came to tell me to move to Houston. Every other order came through the Imams."

I probed, "Where were you headed when we found you?"

"You mean captured me?" Tumbrel interjected. I just nodded.

"I was ordered to go to California and get on a boat, where I would work my way to where I was going. I was told to go to the Philippines and I would be met and told the next step in my journey. So, I don't know where to after that." Tumbrel stated without looking at me. His face turned down to the floor.

"Do you know if anyone is looking for you?" I continued.

"Not yet, I was told to be ready for the one who would meet me on the dock in the Port of Cebu, in the city of Cagayan de Ora. There are several mosques in that city and I was to be met by someone from one of them. That is all I know because the point was to get me out of America and its reach so it was to be a slow trip."

"So, as far as you know, there is no one expecting you yet?"

"That is correct. I was hoping they would send me home for a while before I would come back to work another mission. I have failed completely." Tumbrel mumbled in a flat dejected voice and closing his eyes, laying back down on the cot, "Please just go ahead and kill me because I have failed so badly. Just get it over with."

I stared at the man for several moments and left the room. My team met me in the hall and they stood silent for a moment. Christian voiced their thoughts, "It is a shame that the only answer he has for his situation is to die, shamed and lost forever."

I nodded and sighed, "I wish we could help him to understand that his life doesn't have to be over. Can we pray about it?" Everyone smiled their agreement. I uttered a quick prayer, feeling awkward but the others just grinned and nodded encouragement.

After the prayer, I said, "Based on the information he gave us let's check on any steamer leaving California with stops in that particular port in the last two months, just to cover our bases. We would leave Tumbrel to his misery for now because we didn't want to push quickly and have him block us out like the first couple of weeks. It was a slow process getting him to open up.

Based on the new information, COS Trowbridge ordered the FBI to put the Mosques around the ports of Texas and California under 24/7 surveillance to see who might show up. This coverage would be complete with cameras on buildings and listening devices.

At this point, we went into a waiting pattern, ready to move quickly to where anything of interest might pop up. Most were at home, but Christian and I stayed in DC to continue Tumbrel's interrogation. Dan and Nick went back to Houston where Nick's ties to DHS allowed him to monitor the surveillance of the mosques. We were hoping someone would show up to a local mosque searching for Tumbrel. We were looking for someone who didn't appear on a regular basis. Considering where Tumbrel had told us he was to go, there might not be any action in the near future but our vigilance would be complete. These people had wrought terrible pain and trouble on the people of the

United States and no sacrifice was too much to catch them, especially the "Ghost"!

The others members of the team, hinted that Tanya and I might want to spend some quality time together, while I was up in DC. Their hopes for me were moving right along and it was a running joke with the rest of the team.

It took about a week for our requests for cargo ship names with stops in the Port of Cebu that had left from California ports to arrive from the National Transportation Board. We analyzed it and came up with the sum total of twenty-four ships which left California that had the Philippines as a port of call. Only one had a scheduled traveler that did not arrive before departure. It left the San Diego Port on April 30th headed to the Port of Cebu, the busiest port for travelers. It arrived on May 14th and left again on the 16th for Mumbai (Bombay), India where its travel papers indicated it would return to the Port of Cebu. Our guess based on his statement of wanting to go home, was that Tumbrel would catch a flight out of India, where he could fly to the Domodedoro Airport in Moscow. He could then travel by bus to Chechnya. Our thoughts were his handlers would reward him for his success in the US with a brief rest period at home before calling him back to the fight.

That information gave us a time line of about four and half weeks, so a month more or less. We suspected that when Tumbrel missed his contact in Cebu, the contact in the Philippines would report it to the leader's in the terrorist network, which gave us a timeline of three weeks to set up their surveillance on the Mosques in question, one in Houston and the other in Minneapolis. We, in coordination with the FBI got it set up within two weeks. Everyone concerned had ample incentive to make this work.

Meanwhile, back in D.C., Tumbrel had opened up to me and told me of his travels from Chechnya to the United States, including his time in England learning the basics of real estate and honing his grasp of English. Christian and I were amazed at his willingness to tell us so much about how the system worked to get people into the country. It demonstrated to the entire team, plus everyone in the FBI and DHS working on watching our long borders, one with Canada and one with Mexico, that it wasn't working well for the safety of the American people.

Christian had taken a number of weekend trips home to see his family but I was content to stay in D.C. to spend time with Tanya. We were able to see each other often both on business and for pleasure. During our time together, we discovered a number of likes in common. Our dates together brought us closer with each visit, I finally, but shyly, told Tanya of my acceptance of Jesus as my Lord and Savior. Afterwards, we spent a lot of time going over Bible studies, some suggested by Earnest. Tanya continually thanked the Lord for the quickness of my growth and relationship with the Lord. We both found ourselves more and more enamored with each other.

The day arrived when I had to go home to Alabama and we had a hard goodbye, both declaring this separation was only temporary. We still had jobs to do in two different places but would stay in touch by Skype. I arrived back in the middle of May and began to reorient myself to my normal tasks at work. I did so quickly and was as happy as I had been in a long time. I reconnected with my local family, and was back in the routine of work, MMA, and a new Bible study with my teammates. The team was planning a Memorial Day BBQ get together, enjoying this brief respite from chasing terrorists.

CHAPTER 32

No Rest for the Weary, Memorial Day, Huntsville, Al

Christian and I were sitting together at the holiday BBQ with the rest of the team enjoying the quiet time and avoiding any discussion of our work with the President's COS. We wanted this quiet time with our families to not be tainted by our work undertaken following the attacks of October 10th last year had sent us off many times and directions. Our peace was interrupted when my cell phone rang, Christian and I looked into each other's eyes as I answered. Christian recognized Earnest's voice, and heard the intensity in it. This meant another trip for us.

"John, there was an attempted attack in Cleveland, Ohio. An IED was spotted on the tracks of the local transit company. Fortunately, a vet walking down the tracks recognized it and notified the authorities. They were able to disarm it just in time to avoid a train full of people and saved the day. We have no leads as no one saw who put it there and the police found no physical evidence to follow. I want you and Christian to fly up and check the whole thing out. The local authorities have kept it quiet to avoid creating any panic. They would appreciate your input. Just keep it low key and let me know what you find out. I have alerted the FBI agent in charge of your coming and he will get the ball rolling. I expect it will take about a week for you to talk with everyone since we are keeping this quiet. I'll see you all next week. Sorry to interrupt your weekend off but our enemy doesn't seem to be very considerate." I heard the irony in his voice and didn't comment. He said goodbye and hung up. I looked at Christian and nodded.

We both rose to prepare for our trip. I made my farewells to the group, since I didn't have anyone here to consider and left to grab my go bag. Christian pulled his wife, Eve over and told her of the trip. She just nodded and helped gather his things. She was used to this and knew that her husband was often gone for national security reasons.

CHAPTER 33

The Cleveland Miracle; Cleveland, OH

The day after Memorial Day, Christian and I arrived for a visit with the Cleveland Chief of Police, who appeared surprised to have the local FBI agent bring us to his office. The FBI agent told us, "I worked with the Chief on Memorial Day when all hell almost broke out and I am not sure the Chief will want to talk to you about what he considers a non incident. The Chief appears to be happy it is over and no one was hurt and he wants to keep the city's residents from knowing how close a terrorist attack had come to them."

Upon entering the Chief's office, the FBI agent explained to the Chief, "These men are part of a team that is working on events like this, and the team has been working since the 10/10 aftermath. They are here to follow up only."

The Chief nodded, hesitant, then motioning for me to continue.

I began, "Sir, we understand completely your concerns but our boss is trying to find a way to stop these incidents. If you can arrange it, we would like to interview everyone involved, including the vet."

The Chief, although still hesitant, suggested; "I can coordinate for the responding officer to speak with you and he will contact the vet who discovered that 'thing'. I need you to promise to keep this from the news. I don't want to stir up a panic in my city. Be here in the morning and I will have that interview set up." Christian and I nodded, agreeing to conduct the interviews at the police station and left for our hotel to spend the night.

The following morning, I stood in the police station in Cleveland's downtown area waiting on the patrol officer who had been part of the incident from beginning to end, and considered all the possibilities.

In my mind, I had labeled this 'the Cleveland Miracle,' clearly understanding just how close we had come to a major disaster. The IED was placed on the transit tracks leading to a popular beach on Memorial Day and would have killed a lot of people and injured many more.

Soon, the young patrol officer met me and we moved to a back office where the officer told his story. He started out in a very terse professionally weary manner. "Good morning. Per my report, I was on duty Memorial Day, and about mid morning, I heard running steps behind me. We were all on alert because of DHS's warnings, so I was ready for anything. What I saw was a disheveled man running toward me; wearing a worn out army jacket and waving his arms. I could see he had no weapon in his hands so I, uh, kept my hand on my pistol and waited for him to get to me. At first, it was hard to understand what he was saying; he was so out of breath and talking excitedly. But after a couple of seconds, I gathered that he was a vet, something like EOE and had experience with IEDs and thought he had found one."

"I think you mean EOD" I replied.

"Yeah, that's what he said," the officer continued. "Taking no chances, I followed him to the site and called in the incident. The vet dropped to his knees and began carefully sliding the gravel away from a space between two railroad ties. I tried to stop him, recognizing the possible danger, but he wouldn't stop digging. Then I saw the glint of metal just under the track. I recognized what it was based on some training by the FBI and let my superiors know what we had found. I was sweating bullets so to speak because the transit train was due in about half an hour and there we were."

As the young officer took a deep breath, I considered his information. Christian and I were in the area because of this incident and wanted to ascertain the accuracy of the witnesses. This officer seemed to be well trained and understand the potential impact of an IED exploding in the middle of the festivities for Memorial Day.

I asked the officer, "Did the vet say what he was doing on the tracks?"

"Oh, yes, sir." The officer replied, "He was trying to find his family. Apparently he was discharged after some heavy fighting in Afghanistan. His dad had died while he was deployed and his mom's new address was smeared when he got the letter. I understand it can take a long time for letters to get into Afghanistan. Anyway, he was walking the tracks trying to get to Edgewater Beach, a popular holiday gathering place here in Cleveland. He said he had grown up here and his family always went to the Beach for Memorial Day for the band tributes and BBQ. He was hoping to find someone from his family there. He seems to have had a rough time of it."

"You think his story was real?" I hated to sound cynical but I had to ascertain the intent of everyone involved.

"Oh, yes, sir." The officer said looking at me quizzically. "We did find his family, right there on the Beach just like he'd hoped and they verified his story. O, they didn't know about his struggles after he was discharged or even that he had been discharged. He was having memory problems that prevented him from being able to work long enough to save up enough money to get home. He admitted, his stupid pride had kept him from telling them about his situation. But DHS verified that he was from here and we also contacted the local VA about his case. We had a close call and we consider him a local hero but he refused any publicity, just wanted to be with his family. His mom and sister were thrilled to have him home. The mom had moved in with her sister, who is also a widow, and the vet's sister had recently married and that was why he didn't really know where they lived. Anything else, Sir?"

I simply replied, "No, you have answered all my questions. I have the reports from your bomb squad and other departments. If I need anything else, I'll let your Sergeant know, thank you."

As the officer left the room, I scanned the bomb squad report again and felt I had all I was going to get from here. I would get a better understanding when Christian came back from the forensic lab where he was looking over the device. Christian would be able to make heads and tails over all this bomb mumbo jumbo. He also was waiting for a report from the local DHS who were chasing down the names of any businesses or people in the area that might be suspect.

Christian and I discussed what we might learn beforehand and decided that we would leave the reluctant hero in peace. If they needed to ask more questions later, we knew where he was. After Christian and I discussed our interviews, Christian told me about what he had discovered. "I interviewed the entire bomb squad and they told me about how they raced to disarm the devise in order to beat the coming train. As soon as they had it rendered safe, they moved quickly out of sight as the transit train rolled down the tracks toward them. Only the patrol officer stayed in sight and lots of Clevelanders waved and shouted at him as the train rolled safely down the tracks.

Afterwards, the bomb squad scurried back to carefully gather the explosive device and any material evidence so they could study it back at headquarters. Unfortunately, they did not find fingerprints on the evidence and they had no clue as to just who had planted the device in their city. The whole team was angry, really angry because they knew just how much damage the amount and type of explosive could have done."

Since no one, not even the vet, according to the various reports, saw who had placed the devise on the tracks; the police labeled the case as 'unsolved'. The local authorities thought about it but had no clues to follow. But we would look much deeper into it.

We began a detailed search of any terror fronts or dissidents in the area based on the initial searches by the FBI and DHS. We found some possibilities but only one stood out in our minds. A construction company operating in the area was found to be a subsidiary of the Ferris Construction Company during a very deep computer search. This raised red flags in our minds and we filled in the President's COS, Trowbridge, along with the entire team at the scheduled meeting at the White House.

Christian and I flew directly to D.C.at the end of the week for our team meeting, the other members would join us via VTC.

CHAPTER 34

Constructing the Puzzle

The team met at 6AM in the COS's office in Washington, D.C. We met early or late depending on when everyone was available and there was little traffic in the White House Staff area.

The President's Chief of Staff, Earnest Trowbridge, entered the room nodding to each of us, whispering something special to all seven men and one woman on the team. He liked and respected each of us for our work as his President's 'mighty men'.

He said a quick prayer, starting the meeting with, "Unfortunately, I don't have much. The investigation into our one lead is taking time as the construction company hid its identity deep in a tangled web of legal gobbledygook." I could see the frustration on everyone's face.

"John and Christian, following your report from Cleveland we widened our look at that Ferris Construction Company. It is a large corporation with tentacles spread around the world and it seems that wherever it pops up, nasty things happen. So far, we can only trace it to the mideast. We are still no closer to nailing down anything specific. They have offices all over the world and there seems to be no central place set up as the corporate headquarters, but we are still digging. Meanwhile, as each of you sent detailed reports corroborating its involvement, they are like a ghost, a shadow lurking on the periphery of our vision. I do appreciate all the sacrifices you and your families have made to get us this far. We will meet again when we know more specifics. I know this is frustrating, but we must persevere."

"We understand Sir; it is a privilege to serve." I answered for the group since I had the closest relationship with him. I had served briefly with the President early in his career and knew Earnest from that time.

CHAPTER 35

'The Ghost' Makes Plans

Fletcher Cordell, 'the Ghost' was thinking to himself as he continued his travels through the US. I continue to see the impacts of the Christmas attacks in Boston. The US population, still devastated by these attacks were trying to remain comfortably numb. They were numbing themselves with alcohol and parties celebrating their numerous holidays to block out the possibility of other attacks waiting in the wings. I was a little disappointed with the failed attack in Cleveland, but this was to be expected. I knew the entire US law enforcement were looking for attacks. They had to be right 100% of the time, I just had to succeed every once in a while. I will wear down this country one attack at a time.

I knew the whole Islamic World had also quietly rejoiced in the attacks. I remembered the proud looks in the eyes of the Wraiths when I told them to move to California after Martin had fulfilled his role at the Fire Extinguisher Company. I moved them to add confusion to the Government's attempts to arrest people involved in the attacks and it set them up for their next mission.

I personally notified Martin during a rare visit to the Mosque that they would be moving to California. He wasn't sorry to leave the cold and snow-bound Minnesota for a warmer climate. After that I kept up by reading the weekly reports of the family's journey, compiled by each of my contacts across the country. I was satisfied that they would be the fireworks finale, a spectacular end to this year's round of attacks.

As instructed, Martin left his vehicle with his Imam for disposal, and the family traveled by bus to Indianapolis, IN. There the Imam at the largest Mosque presented the family with new identities, including forged birth certificates, naturalization papers, and driver's license for Martin.

Martin became William Warren, his wife became Marta, and the children received the names, William Junior, or Billy, now nine years old, Chance, now seven years old and little Millie kept her first name since she was only five and a half. All of them started practicing their new names and the parents firmly corrected the kids for mistakes. Little Millie had the hardest time adjusting but after a couple of weeks with neither of her brothers answering her when she used their old names she adjusted too. They had made a game of it all by making rhymes of their new names.

With the pertinent identifications in hand, the family left Indianapolis in an SUV provided by the mosque. It was a brand new adventure for them all and they were happy with the possibilities in front of them. Per our instruction they took five months after 'disappearing' from Minneapolis during the school's winter break in late December to get to California. This allowed them to show up at the end of the school year and avoid questions about where the kids were in school. They arrived in the small town of Aria, between Anaheim and Santa Ana, in late May. William went to work as the assistant manager for a tire company managed by a fellow believer. The Farris

Conglomerate subsidiary purchased a house and it was furnished and ready for them.

Their cover story included that the family homeschooled for religious reasons in hopes of avoiding any unnecessary inquiries. They used this time to grow their faith and learn the details of their mission. Marta purchased family passes to Disneyland Park and during the good weather she took the children multiple times. The children, usually overwhelmed by the number of people, the noise, and the glitter of it all, enjoyed the rides and the food. They ate, played and observed. They stuffed the backpacks with numerous souvenirs to include T-Shirts and hats making sure the backpacks were full. Mostly, they watched the people around them, the security procedures and how Disney ran the park. Marta was appalled by lack of modest dress, the freedom, the constant repugnant behavior of a decadent people. This only re-enforced the idea of their being an instrument of Allah and his judgement. This was their jihad.

At home, the family focused on Allah and the pillars of Islam as a means of helping the boys understand their mission. The children became steeped in the need to advance their religion through any means necessary. Their teachings brought a deeper understanding of the meaning of their heritage and they grew more proud of both their heritage and mission as time passed.

Marta, Billy, Chance and little Millie visited many of the area's attractions but were always home for the little girl's afternoon nap. They bought the boys some Game Boys and they practiced with various games on how to play on them. They had set a solid, quiet routine giving them more time for instruction from the Quran which William taught each night. Occasionally, the Imam visited and tested the boys on their understanding of the Quran encouraging William in his training efforts.

The family continued their habit of Friday prayers in their home. William attended some Friday Prayers at the Mosque with his co-worker but the family lived quietly keeping to themselves. The family used their season tickets freely and grew familiar with all the sites. This was their main activity and their neighbors found their fascination with Disneyland rather charming. In fact, they visited the park so often; some of the staff recognized them and greeted them by name.

CHAPTER 36

Disney's Explosive Light Parade

When Labor Day finally dawned hot and sunny, the Warren family prepared to visit Disneyland. William and I had prepared their plan carefully with some input from the local Imam.

They were to enter the park in the late afternoon to take advantage of the later closing of the Labor Day Weekend. Their season's pass and constant entrances into the park made entry into the park much simpler. The Security officer, who recognized them, waved them on after a cursory inspection of their bags. He even laughed when Millie waved her lollypop. After spending some time walking around the park, they met for a quick prayer and then stationed themselves along the parade route at about eight o'clock to make sure they were near the front of the crowds at the 'hub' for the evening's light parade. The 'Hub is where the statues of Walt Disney and Mickey Mouse stand with Frontierland and Tomorrowland on each side. The evening parade always sailed down Main Street and wound around the Hub exiting into Fantasy Land with its castles and beautiful gardens.

Marta and Millie moved amongst the crowd at Fantasy Land directly across from the Hub. Millie's part was simple, run out and hand her lollypop to one of the princess characters on a float holding on tightly to the stick. Billy centered himself in the midst of the people gathered at Frontier Land, apparently engrossed in the game in his hand, the crowd undulating around him, pushing for a better view of the parade. William and Chance pushed into the center of the Tomorrow Land crowd. People always crowded into the small area that surrounds the parade route, creating a solid mass of folks surrounding the Hub. We expected the area to be packed and William texted me a smiley face to let me know the plan was on target.

The parade started down Main Street and filled the area with lights and sound. As it circled the Hub, Marta watched with pride as Millie pushed through the indulgent crowd and started her dash toward the float. Millie's part was the simplest; hand the 'lollypop' to one princess on the float, making sure she held on tight in order to pull the stick out of her 'lollypop" which was designed to detonate the C-4 painted to look like candy and covered in cellophane. As Millie reached the float and handed up her 'lollypop', a smiling princess took hold of the lollipop and Millie pulled the stick.

As Millie ran forward, the rest of the Warren family shouted 'Ala Akbar' and triggered their devices. The stunned crowd at first turned to look for who had shouted the all too familiar phrase, when everyone was suddenly knocked down by explosions from multiple sources which rocked the entire area of the 'Hub'. In that terrible instant, the Happiest Place on Earth, became the Evil Queen's fiery landscape.

The loud music and the noise of the crowd muffled the initial sounds of explosions, but nothing could drown out the screams of terror and pain. Those close to detonations or in the kill zone, were knocked over, some going airborne, with even more riddled with metal and bone shrapnel.

Surviving family and friends let out a howl of frustration, fear, anger, and sorrow as they started to get up covered with debris, blood, and other body parts. When the realization of what had happen hit the crowd, a stampede of people rushing up Main Street seeking safety generated a mob scene. Those who had been closest to any member of the Warren family were now only part of the smoking black scorches on the pavement. Shrieks of anguish rose in the evening air where only moments before, the sound of Disney magic was heard.

Park Security and every available employee rushed into action trying to contain the fear crazed visitors from trampling one another in their rush away from the smoke and flames.

Despite Disney's best efforts, the mass of the crowd ended up causing the trampling deaths of several guests and a couple of employees. The beautiful parade float and shrubbery closest to the explosions caught fire. Hundreds of people collapsed, pushed by the force of the explosions and several guests clothing was on fire. Their panic only increased the push of the crowd to escape.

The center of the Hub was being inundated with the burning parts of the scenery. The debris from the destructive force of four bombs was drifting about like a messy, colorful snow fall. Children snatched up and carried by hysterical parents' cried hot tears of panic, echoing their parents who were unaware of the scalding tears pouring down their faces.

Disney quickly called 911 and started their protocols for this type of event by setting up numerous first aid stations and sending out employees to find anyone they could help. The Anaheim police on duty at the Park called for backup, police, fire, and medical. The hub was dotted with scorched or burning shrubbery or melting plastic. The float that previously held smiling princesses was burning and the metal framework was wilting. There was no sign of any princesses in the area.

I watched with wonderment at another successful attack on the infidels as coverage crossed the world in mere moments.

CHAPTER 37

Labor Day Chaos

Shortly after eleven pm on Labor Day, my phone rang, it was Earnest, who told me, "Turn on your TV!" I turned on the TV and was startled when I heard the Disneyland Park Manager begin to give an interview.

In a flat tone, the Park Manager began, "Evening, thank you for coming to this press brief. I was in the Park when this terrible event once again marred another national holiday. We at Disney have instituted our security protocols put in place despite our hope never to have to use them. Disney is a family institution, based on accepting everyone in the spirit of Walt Disney. For the first time in Disney history, we had to implement a crowd control method set up for such an incident. We are still trying to ascertain what happened during the evening light parade. We are still gathering information, but I will brief you on what we currently know, with the caveat that all our information is only partial at this time. All I can tell you at this time is that there were several confirmed deaths in the park. I have no further information at this time on what caused the deaths, but we are investigating the incident with local law enforcement. Families seeking information on their loved ones can call the number listed at the bottom of the screen, but I warn you that most of the information we have is sketchy at best. Please be patient as we try to sort out the confusion. We are doing all that we can at this time. We have set up a command center with local law enforcement agencies to direct our efforts, to include setting up several medical triage centers. Our Emergency staff is asking that any guests, especially doctors or nurses to go to one of the command points and let us know you are willing to assist the park at this time. I have been in touch with the Anaheim Chief of Police who has notified all appropriate agencies in order to assist Disney in handling this crisis. Disney and its employees are grieving the loss of life…and the damage to 'happiest place on the earth' forever."

I watched as the spokesman try to control his voice and emotions in the very difficult circumstances and then sighed as he continued.

"I will not answer any questions at this time. The next brief will come from the lead officer in charge. Disney will keep everyone informed about the scheduling of the next brief."

Earnest quickly told me, "Get your team to Disneyland ASAP. We are now preparing to return to the White House. I want the whole team on site in California. The President is so angry that I'm praying he won't have a stroke. I'll be praying for all of you too. I've got to go, I have a call which shows it is from DHS, who are probably calling me to officially notify me and the president. I am the first call after DHS learns of any situation like this, I will call you later if I get any more details."

I was on the internet skyping with Tanya when the call from Ernest had come in, she had stayed on the skype call and heard the entire discussion. Her phone rang and again it was Earnest. She raised her finger asking for a moment, as she talked on her phone. I heard her say, "Yes, Sir, I'll be right over." She then turned back to me and said, "John, Earnest wants to talk to everyone via VTC. Since I was already talking with you, he said to tell you and the team to go to the secure conference room at AMC (Army Materiel Command) headquarters. He's already spoken with the Commander and it is all set. I am to meet him at the White House conference room in about half an hour so we will all be available to consider what we want to do. I'll see you then."

I murmured, "OK" and we both hung up. I immediately called Christian, and using the groups standard operating procedures (SOP), we each call the other four, two each. I called Nick Forrest who was in the middle of settling into his new apartment just off Rideout Road. They had about twenty-five minutes to call and get to AMC headquarters. I gave a quick thanks that everyone was in town this Labor Day.

As the teleconference began, Trowbridge brought everyone up to speed on what exactly was fact and I said, "Sir, we will make definite plans to," Trowbridge stopped me mid-sentence with, "I have already spoken with the Redstone Arsenal Commanding General, and the Commanding General of the Alabama Air National Guard, who is arranging for a flight for you to California; it will be ready in about an hour. The President and I are leaving on Marine One within minutes to Andrews Air Force Base to head that way as well. We will make a secure call to you at the park office. I have arranged for a secure communication through DHS in the park."

I said quietly, "yes, sir." Ernest hung up the phone. We each left for home to grab our go bags. Each of the seven of us had grown used to these sudden trips since the terrible 10/10 attacks. This was not as usual for Nick Forrest, our DHS assistant, but at this rate, he would soon be up to speed.

As it turned out, everyone was on board within the hour. The plane took off as we discussed all that had happened during this terrible fall season. I said, "Let's go over what has happen adding in the new information from the past months. Following swiftly on the heels of the 10/10 attacks, there was the absolute failure of the Iowa mission at the terrorist camp with terrible losses to the FBI and ATF. Then there was the attack in Atlanta on Black Friday. We hoped for an end but then came the Sarin attacks at the Christmas programs at the two most famous presentations in Boston, staples of the Christmas season in the U.S. Let's not forget the attempt in Cleveland on the 4th of July. Thankfully an alert veteran noticed an IED on the tracks in Cleveland. It was set to explode when a trolley car full of celebrating Ohioans came down the tracks and was only averted by minutes. The US is already on edge. And now this, this is unthinkable! The United States is being attacked in so many ways."

A general babble of anger, frustration, and downright desire to hurt someone filled the plane.

Marcus Owens, the retired Green Beret officer, was the quiet one of the bunch. A tall, rugged black man, he was often the one who pondered while the others tossed out scenarios for the situation facing them. He sat hunched down in his seat while the others just railed at this outrage.

Suddenly Marcus pushed up in his seat and said, "Guys, think for a moment." Since he was the quiet one, when he spoke, the others immediately hushed and listened. "These things have been happening all fall. He restated what I had covered, saying," these attacks have been on uniquely

American holidays except for 10/10. This looks to me like direct attacks on everything American, but more specifically on special occasions as part of the heritage or on facilities important to our way of life. What do you think?"

The six others sat for a moment and I raised my hand in salute to Marcus. "I think Marcus has hit the nail on the head. It was hard to see until now although Trowbridge has brought that up with Christian and I, but these are all holidays or iconic events or places in the U.S. that are pretty much at the heart of America. Northeast, Mid-west, Southwest, and now the West coast and Disneyland! We need to look at this with a new perspective. Maybe we can determine other possibilities and hopefully head off some with a bit of thought and cautionary planning. At least I hope so!"

The teleconference from Air Force One Secure Room was brief and to the point. Earnest updated our team with the little he knew and said, "We can only deal with what we know for sure and I want you all on this situation, you are my eyes and ears for anything like this. Do any of you have any questions?" I asked, "Is our media relations person coming as well?"

Earnest replied, "No, not now, I want her in DC for any media questions and there will be plenty for sure. We will begin to formulate a statement based on what we know and perhaps anything the team can tell us of as you get there. I think time is of the essence and it will be easier for us to collaborate by secure phones. Now, let's roll. It will be very late when you arrive, so try and rest on the flight. I want you to go straight to the scene when you arrive. God go with you!"

Christian nudged me saying, "Tough luck buddy!"

CHAPTER 38

The Puzzle Starts to Form

On the way, we watched the next press briefing from Disneyland. The Chief of Police strode out from the entrance toward the gathering media in the parking lot area.

"Ladies and gentlemen of the press, thank you for responding to this tragedy. All I can tell you as of now is that the area is in chaos and there is still uncertainty about what really happened. As I understand right now, we combined with Disney's Head of Security believe that several suicide bombs were detonated in the midst of the crowd enjoying the evening light parade. Our information is still preliminary. We are trying to determine what is real and what is speculation. We have finally settled all the guests and are moving them through the interview process and moving them to secure locations as quickly as possible.

The explosions did little damage to the structures in the Park, the area of the incident was crowded with guests wanting to see the parade, so our guests took the brunt of the attack.

We can confirm the death of several people during the initial attack but we are still trying to ascertain the full extent of the impact on the park and personnel. We would like to thank the physicians and nurses on staff, as well as some great volunteers from the guests who are currently attending the injured. We have ambulances on site to transport the injured. We are also aware of the possibility of concussive injuries. So, for now, we are doing what we can do and I will try to keep you informed but our first duty is to our guests and their families. Please do not interfere with staff or police who are dealing with a very tough situation. Thank you." He did not answer any questions or acknowledge those shouted at him but returned to the work inside the park.

Our arrival was so 'normal' that no one really noticed as we flew into the John Wayne Airport in Anaheim. The Air National Guard jet Earnest had arranged for already knew the drill and since this was a big Airport for Hollywood no one paid the least attention to another jet landing. We picked up the van reserved for us and Christian drove toward Disneyland. There was a short wait until the local DHS agent was contacted to escort us directly to the Town Hall building. We introduced ourselves and got down to business.

DHS Agent Mitchell began the briefing, knowing we had been sent by the President. "Since our last call to Washington, the area has cooled down enough for us to start setting up a grid search and documentation. We have also begun questioning the witnesses. We moved everyone to a secure area. Disney has graciously allowed us to use the train station for triage and town hall buildings as medical facilities, where the medical staff checks everyone out. We segregated the families who lost loved ones, while we started questioning everyone else from the area for witness statements. The majority of those interviewed only knew that people had been killed in the blasts at the end of the parade and that others were injured during the aftermath."

Kevin Williams, Disney Head of Security added, "Moving the family members with lost loved ones was the most difficult. In shock and disbelief, they wanted to stay there hoping this was a terrible nightmare. It took a great deal of compassion and firmness to finally move these to the command area for medical evaluation. We have these families set up in the main room at Town Hall. We have practiced for these scenarios regularly and sadly it is paying off.

When we were finally able to meet with the family members of those killed or at least missing, it was much more difficult. It took much longer as many just began to cry, were confused or in denial. Disneyland security and the Anaheim Police are still combing the park for people who might be in hiding or just lost in the many nooks or crannies, hoping some of those unaccounted for were tucked away afraid but safe.

Even though we are as frustrated and upset as the civilians, we also know that the first information given often proves the most valuable. Of course, when the emotional turmoil dies down, more concrete information might be forth coming. So far that is the extent of anything solid. This is a terrible incident and will send the nation into a greater panic and perhaps anger. I myself am having difficulty with not wanting to hit something, hard!"

As we integrated ourselves, details were slowly emerging and soon a pattern began to emerge from the scrambled reports. Apparently, one or two people had placed themselves in the center of the crowds around the 'hub' and shouted 'Ala Akbar' just after a small girl ran out in the street holding something toward a princess on a float. As whatever she had handed to the princess blew up, corresponding blasts took place in each of the entrances to the 'Lands' of Disney.

No one could definitively tell who did the deed but those standing near each 'land' described a different person. Depending on where they had been standing, they described a man and young boy, a woman, or a ten or eleven-year-old boy. All the witness statements only agreed on one fact that the small girl, guessed to be four or five, ran up to the Princess float to hand something to one of the actresses initiated the attack and that all the bombers seemed to have dark hair and complexion. The girl's dash set off the explosions. The consistency of these reports began to form the idea of a family."

We, the FBI, DHS, and Anaheim Police were beginning to think the unthinkable. A whole family had come into the park and done this? A Family? Children? Adults, Ok, but Children? What kind of parent would urge their child to do this kind of thing?

Even we found it hard to swallow that 'loving' parents could bring their children to such an end. But, as one soldier commented, "it's not without precedent within certain regions. Even in Iraq, children were given live hand grenades and told to give it to the 'nice' soldier. There had been a lot of negative coverage when one of the children was shot before getting close enough to harm the soldier. In other 'wars', soldiers died because of certain rules of engagement forced on them by people who had no idea of the evil our enemies are capable of or the realities of war.

The crime scene was such a mess, slowing down the investigation, the large panicked crowds contaminated the scene. The Anaheim CSI concentrated on trying to find human DNA that could possibly help them identify the culprits and victims. It didn't offer much hope in our minds but it was the best they had. So the painstaking work of scraping each area began. The number of small number signs around kept growing as they scraped, put down a sign, and then photographed each place.

The scrapings went from the outside of the blast circle inwards with an occasional body part, arm, leg, or even only a hand being found at the edges of the blackened areas. We felt sure that most would be contaminated by samples of several sets of DNA from the force of the blasts. Because the intensity of the blasts and the spatter pattern from the blasts covered a large area, the work was tedious and time consuming. Add to that there were four areas of explosive remnants, from the floats, the areas directly in front of the entrances to Frontier Land, Fantasy Land, and Tomorrow Land. Only people who had actually visited Disneyland were aware of how small an area it really was. This meant that the outward force of the blasts almost covered the entire area of the hub.

The work in the lab became almost mind numbing and the lab team was growing increasingly weary when additional crime scene investigators from DHS, FBI, and the military arrived to help. Earnest Trowbridge was calling in all of his resources. The locals were sent to rest after giving a detailed report on the investigations underway, following specific protocols. Late in the night, one investigator gave a loud yelp that shattered the quiet. Everyone looked up as he shouted, “I have found a match!”

It turned out to be a male of mid-eastern descent and his DNA was on file as a worker in a fire extinguisher manufacturer. This was our only lead at this point and it was put on the fast track.

CHAPTER 39

Connecting the DNA Dots

Later the next day, FBI Agent Jason Carson called our command center at Disneyland. He reported the following, "I went to the owner's office of the small Fire Equipment Company and asked for their file on Martin Wraith. The owner's secretary was looking through her files and finally came up with the matching file. Martin Wraith fits the profile, but he disappeared without a trace during the school break around the Christmas holiday. During my earlier visit with both you and Christian, I remembered several men mentioning the man as being a floor supervisor before his disappearance. There had been some confusion for a short period of time when he left without giving notice, leaving no one in charge which is why they said they remembered so clearly. The new supervisor took over and quickly smooth everything out. No one had a clue as to what had happened to the Wraith family but since the company had changed hands so soon afterwards, it was forgotten.

The company reported their disappearance but the police found no clues when they searched the Wraith house. It appeared to have been professionally cleaned to the point that it appeared as if no one had ever lived there.

According to state ID records, Wraith had a wife and three children, two boys and a girl. It had been a puzzle but with no possible explanation, the police finally dropped the case into the unsolved/cold case file and their disappearance was soon forgotten. Wraith had been given a DNA test as part of the company policy when he was hired about six years ago. It was on file but the rest is a mystery. There was enough going on that no one ever made the connection to the terrorist's attacks.

After Agent Carson completed his call, Christian and I almost high fived each other. This information fit our profile information so strongly, along with the team's knowledge that this company had been the supplier for the fire extinguishers used in Boston; the connection was a sure thing in our minds. The question was, where and how did this family get to California and at Disneyland and how did the use of the children fit the pattern of the other attacks? Although the terrorists at the school outside Washington had forced a young boy to answer the phone, no children were specifically used by the terrorist in the 10-10 attacks.

The idea of a family moving silently and stealthily across country to commit such a heinous attack fit the picture of the terrorists to a T, a capital T! The question became, what good knowing this would do in the investigation? If all of them were dead, there might be no chance of following-up.

I looked at the CSI Lead Investigator and suggested, "I want you to focus on the DNA found near where the float was destroyed. See if you can find a familiar match to the one confirmed by Agent Carson. That little girl is consistent across everyone's statements from the scene. It could also be a good thing to try and match any possible DNA from the center of each of the blast sites. This might, the

Good Lord willing, tie down the idea of a family. I know that thought is repugnant for everyone, but we must confirm or deny this as a fact. Nick, can DHS learn where the parents are from?" Nick replied, "I will check." "Great" I said, "Get back to us as quickly as possible."

The reports started coming in and the careful work and diligence of the CSI's finally yielded some information. The amount of DNA from the suspected bombers was small but enough remained to make a tentative match with the woman and the children including where the Princess float exploded. The children had a familial match to Martin Wraith and we were able to match the children's mitochondrial DNA to the woman, confirming they were a family. The local police began a careful search of Disney files about a family that matched what little they could deduce from the eye witness accounts and found one family that matched all the indicators. The William Warren family.

I received daily updates from all the agencies. We discovered that William Warren worked at a tire company whose manager had also disappeared during the Labor Day weekend. Upon getting a home address from his employer, we went to his residence and confirmed DNA matches with Martin Wraith and his family.

Local law Enforcement conducted interviews with the neighbors and reported that their comments were telling and consistent. "Why, they seemed nice enough, pretty much kept to themselves but we all thought it was cute that they were fascinated with Disneyland." They stepped back in horror as the questioners indicated that the family might be tied to the events at Disneyland. Each one stammered a chorus of, "They have only lived here since the summer began. They were always off to some sight or another but most often to Disneyland. Oh, oh, no.... One family told us that they had planned to be at Disneyland for that evening but a last minute call saying the wife's mother had taken a turn for the worse sent them to Los Angeles instead. They praised God that she had recovered quickly after her family arrived!"

I shook my head as the lead investigators told me of the interviews and the reactions of the local people. "This always devastates those who live near the terrorists and don't have a clue. I wish all our citizens would be open to possibilities. After 9/11, that awareness was there but it only lasted a short time. We all need to be aware and watchful. Like the Sherriff in Texas said, 'Better to be wrong than sorry.'"

CHAPTER 40

Investigation at the Pace of Molasses in January

After some tedious and time consuming leg work, we came up with the conclusion that the Warren/Wraith house was bought and furnished by a local company. I asked the team to dig further into that company to see if it was a subsidiary of foreign companies. Christian and I had a feeling that the Ferris Conglomerate would eventually show up.

We kept this to ourselves per Trowbridge's instruction even though we felt it a bit unfair to the local police. The team gathered for a teleconference every day for a week but then we held them as needed. The others called home almost daily to keep up with their families, none of us could really discuss the details of the investigation. Christian razed me about my daily conversations with Tanya, "Hey you can at least talk to her about what's happening here!" I said with a sheepish grin, "We're not talking shop!" He laughed and said, "I bet not, you love birds!" Bringing a flush to my face that had the rest of the team laughing in a knowing manner with me.

We remained in California for another week, keeping tabs on the investigation's progress. The process moved into the grinding snail pace of picking apart every clue, every thought, every 'gut' feeling. This was the grunt work of investigation and they had small victories and a lot of dead ends. It was finally determined by the Immigration and Naturalization people that the family originally came from The United Arab Emirates. The man, Martin Wraith, had come to the U.S. about six years before and was married with two sons when he arrived. There were no hints of what the family's original name was. Beyond that, the whole family remained a mystery. Encouraging your own children to kill themselves with an explosive device was still a horrifying thought to everyone who had a hand in the investigation.

With Earnest's blessing, we headed home to Alabama with promises on all sides to keep each other informed of any new information that came to light. It was frustrating to everyone that the pace was so slow because everyone wanted to solve this now! But like in so many of these cases, it was the slow, steady, piece by piece, putting together of the puzzle that led to capturing the culprits.

Back in Alabama during our workouts together, the group frequently discussed the company that kept popping up in all their investigations. The ownership was shrouded in a black hole of corporate loopholes and subsidiaries that we asked Nick Forest of DHS and Earnest to widen the searches to foreign nations.

Nick was finally settled in to his new job at the Huntsville DHS Office. He was enjoying being with the team and our interaction. He had even joined us in our exercise program, but was doing a bit of 'catching up' on the intensity.

Everyone else's families were excited to have them home, and each of them were bombarded by their children with lots of questions about what was Disneyland like or were Mickey and Minnie all right. Each of them told their children that the two famous mousers were ok but refrained from going into too much detail. In fact, Christian had asked the actors who played them to autograph a picture, delighting his children, who wanted it framed and hung on the wall. Christian happily hung it on the kitchen wall. He had asked for an identical picture for the other men's children and would give them to their kids as a special gift.

A month after arriving home, we stood in the gym to give thanks for the quiet six weeks. We hoped that this was over, at least for now, but no one seriously thought it was. Each of us carried a slight bitter taste in our mouths knowing somewhere deep inside that it was not over.

Nick and I settled into the routine of going to work daily and plenty of work was required as Redstone Arsenal had the unenviable position of being high on the list of foreign intelligence operatives, due to all the major technical and space programs located in the area.

As October and early November passed by with no incidents, the bitter fear in our thoughts started to diminish. No one was thinking it was really over but perhaps it was a long lull in terrorist activity.

Tonya made arrangements to visit me over the Thanksgiving weekend to meet my siblings and her family. I was going to Birmingham to meet her family. It was a big step for both of us and I alternated between excitement and fear of being disliked on sight. We encouraged each other that nothing could be further from the truth.

CHAPTER 41

Meeting the Family Southern Style

Tonya called me late Wednesday night telling me of her arrival in Birmingham. "I was met by my parents and they took me to a local restaurant where my only sister remained quiet despite smiling at my dad's and brothers' teasing me the entire time. To my dismay, a number of people came to our table to ask for my autograph. My family enjoyed watching me blush from all the attention. They also teased me about finally bringing a 'beau' home to meet the family. But they were all happy for me and we laughed the entire evening."

On Thursday, her family gathered again and the teasing continued as they waited for me to show up for the big dinner. When I got there the whole house smelled like Thanksgiving with turkey, dressing, and several kinds of pies ready and waiting, all the Southern standards for this particular meal.

I arrived early and waited five minutes to make sure I arrived right on time. I did see Tanya peeking out the window as I waited the five extra minutes. I knew she was laughing to herself about military men and their on-time is late, early is on time and heaven forbid you are ever late attitude. My military training was on full display. All the guys on the team had regaled her with stories of arriving five minutes early and waiting to knock on the door at precisely the time designated on the invitation. Punctuality meant arriving at the very moment stated on the invitation.

I went up and rang the doorbell and Tanya's father opened the door and grinned. He gave me a hearty handshake, I shook the hand back looking him straight in the eyes, standing tall, just like all my training had instilled in me. It was important in a father's eyes.

I was ushered into the house, momentarily taken aback by the rush of people wanting to shake my hand. But in only a moment, the lady of the house, Tanya's mother, shooed them all away and enveloped me in a bear hug. Tanya just laughed and mouthed, "Welcome to the south!" Tanya's mom said, "Welcome John, you go into the den and talk sports with the men, as we get the final fix'ns done."

I moved into the den and we soon were talking about the big game tomorrow, and I was able to chime in with some thoughts. I was not from Alabama, but few people in the U.S. did not know of the fierce rivalry between the University of Alabama and Auburn University and the famous Iron Bowl. In fact, when I first arrived at Redstone, I was asked who I rooted for, Alabama or Auburn? I looked confused until my boss said, "Son in Alabama, you got to choose a side."

Dinner was delightful and I found her family charming, if a bit rambunctious. They seemed happy to meet me and I caught a number of slight jabs at Tanya for my presence. Apparently, she had never brought a man to the house since high school. I wondered about that a bit since she was so beautiful, intelligent, funny, and a lovely companion. I would ask her later about that, but for now, it was just all fun.

After the meal was finished, Tanya and her mother cleared the table with the help of the brothers, and her dad and I went to sit on the front porch. Her dad quietly rocked for a while and I waited quietly on pins and needles.

Finally, her dad said, "What do you think of all these attacks in our country?"

I was so surprised that it took me a moment to rearrange my thoughts. "Well, they seem to be well coordinated and an attack on all things American."

Mr. Anderson nodded, "Just what I have been thinking, but others just seem immune to that reality."

I nodded, "Yes sir, it is a shame."

"Tanya tells me that you are working with her and some others on finding the source of these attacks. What exactly does that look like? She is almost secretive about what she does. Oh, we see her on the television a lot, but she doesn't talk about what you all do. She mentioned a number of other men." He paused looking at me.

I stared at the house across the street as I considered my answer. "We are investigating the attacks and working on ways to hopefully preempt any others. We work from Huntsville and with all the agencies. You know, DHS, FBI, all the 'letter agencies.' Tanya works with the agencies and the White House on the communications end of things."

Mr. Anderson nodded and commented, "You can't tell us about it, can you?"

"No sir."

"So tell me how you met my daughter and a bit about yourself."

I swallowed hard and began my rehearsed spiel. "I met your daughter just after the 10/10 attacks in Chicago. She was the first person we interviewed after the attack on the Chicago Mercantile Exchange. Since then we have worked on several other incidents together." Mr. Anderson gave a small huff, and said, "Son, take a breath. I don't shoot on holidays."

This enlisted a strained laugh from me, but I nodded and continued. "I am originally from North Carolina, raised up in the mountains in a small town west of Asheville, Waynesville, North Carolina. I joined the Army ROTC program in college, receiving my commission and went active duty. I was married before but my wife died in a weird car accident while I was deployed to Iraq. It has taken me a good while to get over that, but I recently realized with some help from a friend that she would not want me to walk alone forever. She loved the Lord and would want me to move on. I also just recently asked the Lord to come into my life and I believe this has prepared me to move past that tragedy. I attended church with my wife. She liked it so much, but it never was that big in my life at the time. Now it is, thanks to my friends and your daughter. I guess that's about it." My heart was beating fast as I considered what I would want to know about a man taking up with my daughter, should I ever have one.

The quiet seemed to shout at me as Tanya's father just rocked and stared into space. He finally spoke, "Does your work place you in much danger? Could it place my daughter in danger?"

"No sir, except maybe the travel. It's pretty cut and dried."

"Uh, hum. Let's go in. They will be finished up in there and ready for more talk and T.V."

We rose from the rockers and entered the house where the brothers had the T.V. on and were listening to all the pregame talk. There was a lot of banter about the game.

Tanya soon joined me on the sofa and reached out for my hand, whispering, "Not too bad, I hope." I shook my head no, whispering back, "Can we talk later?"

The plan was for Tanya to ride to Huntsville with me and stay with Christian's family at night and then return on Saturday.

Wanting to get to Huntsville before it was too late; we left about six and arrived at Christian's house about seven. We talked on the trip, and finally Tanya assured me that the conversation was typical of her dad. No worries about that.

After Christian's wife Eve welcomed Tanya warmly, she seemed to relax a bit. She had worked with the team for about a year but had never met any of their wives. This was a whole new realm of relationship that was probably a bit scary for her. These people had been through a lot together and she was the "new kid on the block," so to speak.

After a light supper and a lively interchange on the news, everyone retired for the evening, after I left at about eleven. No one had to get up early, but Eve laughed that her youngest was always up with the birds.

CHAPTER 42

The Iron Bowl Turns Molten

After all, this was the weekend in Alabama, the annual football game for bragging rights for the year. Alabama and Auburn are among the fiercest rivalries in the nation, and families, towns, and the whole state lived for this game. Alabama retailers had orders in place for the shirts giving the final score and would have them in stores on Monday. The game was on the Saturday after Thanksgiving and short of the actual thanksgiving dinner, nothing held the state attention like the game.

I arrived to share breakfast and plan out the day. I planned to take Tanya to the sites of interest on the Arsenal and in the town. As they were starting out, my phone rang and I reluctantly answered it.

My smile turned to a frown as I listened to Earnest Trowbridge. I turned the car around and drove back to Christian's place, a deep frown on my face. Tanya raised her eyebrows but said nothing.

"Christian, I need to talk with you," I shouted racing up the front stairs. "We need to go to Tuscaloosa!" Christian arrived at the door with the newspaper in his hand and a question mark on his face. "What is it? Oh, come on in."

I tugged Tanya in with me and settled her on the couch. "I just got a call from Earnest and there is a situation in Tuscaloosa. A bunch of specialty seats at the stadium just blew up. They are talking with everyone, but it's the day before the game and they are concerned and the COS wants the whole team there ASAP. We need to call everyone, and Tanya, since you are here, he wants you to go also. Since this game is a media frenzy, he feels your presence can help defuse some of the rumors. Anyway, there's a student involved and Earnest wants our input as quickly as possible. Tanya, can you gather your things here and I will call my guys while Christian calls his. Plan on staying for at least a couple of days. See you shortly." With that, I rushed out the door, turning back to say, "Tanya, call your parents. We have no idea how long we will be at the University."

Within twenty minutes, all the men and their cars were at Christian's house. The team divided themselves into two vehicles; one was Dan's van that carried five comfortably, and my car. Tanya and I would drive over together, and she could happily say that this would not be uncomfortable like our ride in Houston.

We arrived at Bryant-Denny Stadium and were allowed through the police line once we showed ID, apparently Earnest had called ahead. We met with the site commander, CPT Bullock gave us a brief on what he knew at the time.

"This morning, we got a call from some tailgaters about smoke and explosions coming from inside the stadium. SGT Carpenter started questioning the fans, I had other responders set up a perimeter as the firemen raced into the stadium. The firemen reported that there were multiple fires at various places in the seats sections of the stadium. Their chief called for back up. These were already on the way because anything that happened at the University was of importance to everyone in the town. The tornado that had ripped through the area several years earlier with a number of deaths had created an acute attitude of readiness in all the responders.

Police approached a number of the folks around the parking area. All of them pointed to Jerry and he became the center of our attention. Our lead detective pulled the student away from the crowd and into an alcove entrance from the parking area. Here is SGT Carpenter who interviewed the kid involved." SGT Roy Carpenter stepped up, cleared his throat and started.

"I interviewed Jerry Nolen and here is what he told me, He was flying a Quad Copter he built for one of his classes and then heard some explosions in the stadium. Smoke began to rise and then a bunch of tailgaters ran toward him, all looking up. Smoke began to seep over the sides and I heard the sound of fire truck sirens. a few of the more aggressive fans growled at him, "What did you do?" among the other questions.

I watched Jerry as I questioned him, looking at his demeanor and any indications of possible lies. I found no evidence of ill will but a lot of fear and consternation in the boy's recounting. I also learned that his family lived in the area. I informed him that we would need the controller and the plane. Sgt. Carpenter spoke up, "We have interviewed both Jerry and his dad, plus the FBI also made a call on them. Something this strange happening the day before the big game when the stadium would be filled with over a hundred thousand people was beyond what we wanted to tackle alone. So, Chief of Police Stan Middleton called in for extra help."

CHAPTER 43

T-Town Investigation

After our initial canvas and interviews we went to the University President office per Earnest's instructions. There were a number of people just standing around on their cell phones. The tension level was so thick you could cut it with a knife. People not on phones alternated between wringing their hands and whispering to each other.

I asked to speak with the person in charge and was immediately shown to the man in sports clothes on the far side of the area, identified as the DHS agent. We moved in unison toward the DHS Agent, the crowd moving aside as we strode past them.

"Sir, we are the team from Redstone Arsenal and we were told to talk with you. My name is John Banks and we are the ones working for Mr. Trowbridge. Can we get 'read in' so that we are working at the same level of knowledge as you?"

The agent stared at me and then ran his eyes over the team and said, "Well, hello Nick, what are you doing in Alabama? Last I heard you were caught up in the mess in Las Vegas."

Nick laughed as he said, "That would be correct, but now the powers that be have moved me to Redstone Arsenal and I work closely with this team."

"Well good. Let's go into the President's office and I will get ya'll up to speed, not that we know much right now."

Once in the room, he gave us a full rundown of what he knew for certain, the bare facts that they had ascertained so far. It wasn't much. I asked if we could talk with the student.

"Sure thing. I'll arrange for you to speak with him. His name is Jerry Nolen. He is a student in the electrical engineering school and I understand that his hope is to develop an undetectable way of guiding unmanned planes. Do you need to have anyone check out the stadium?"

I replied, "Christian is our EOD guy and I'd like him to take at least one of the guys with him. I understand it's a big stadium and a decision must be made soon."

So I decided to send Christian and Dan to the stadium and Tanya and I would go to the student's house. In the meantime, the agent in charge would notify the student's family of our arrival.

The agent said, "I can make that all happen. I would appreciate your other men looking at the paper work we have been able to get hold of on short notice. A lot of people who would have easy access were out of town for the holiday, but I do understand that most of them are on their way back. No one from the University misses this game."

The men all left to attend to their assignments, the group going through papers looking for a specific name, but figured it would take a deeper level search than the University had at their disposal to find the illusive conglomerate name. But this was part of investigating and they had a deeper knowledge of the probable terrorists. Fortunately, they had Nick and the whole DHS to help.

It took about ten minutes to reach the student's home. As they drove down the street, Tanya took my hand and gently asked the Lord for wisdom and understanding for this event. I just nodded and kept my eyes on the road.

We were cordially invited in to the Nolen home by Jerry's mom. We asked to have a brief discussion about what happened and she said, "They came in to tell me what was going on. I was all nervous about what happen after Charles got a call from Jerry. Of, course, there wasn't much they could tell me as they only knew that something had happened with Jerry's helicopter and it looked like something bad.

I sank down in the couch as they told the tale. "What does all this mean?" was all I could say."

Charles stepped up and said, "Diane, we don't know anything more. The FBI came and if my guess is right, we'll be dealing with Homeland Security as well. Certainly looks strange on the day before the big game, so many people at the stadium and Jerry said it sounded like explosions and I could still smell the arid smoke when I got there."

I spoke softly, "Thank you for letting us come to your home and talk about what has happened. We work for the President. First of all, let me say that we only want to know the facts from your son's perspective; there is no evidence that he has done anything other than expose a potential terrorist attack at the game tomorrow. So, in a way, he is a hero, but we don't want you inundated with hoards of reporters and such."

Jerry's father seemed to relax a bit, but still looked shell shocked, as did Jerry, who was hovering slightly behind his parents. "I don't know if there is much we can tell you that we haven't already told the police and FBI."

I nodded but assured him, "We are looking for a different perspective, and perhaps by now, your son can answer some questions that were not part of the original interviews."

The father nodded and indicated they all sit down.

"Jerry, that is your name, right?" The boy nodded a bit fearful of all the attention. "Well, we won't keep you long. We just have a few questions, ok? Just tell us what happened."

Jerry nodded hesitantly and began to speak. "As my quad-copter soared, I decided to send it up over the stadium to test its height capabilities. I was thrilled by its immediate response to my commands. I watched it soar up and over the side of the stadium. I then made it make a left turn, then another left turn, and like a NASCAR race another left so it made a complete circle above the stadium. Then I signaled it to descend back to right in front of me. As I finished the route, I heard explosive sounds rocket off the sides of the stadium.

Then Jerry nodded and spread out his hands to indicate that he had no idea how he could help them any further. I just smiled and Jerry relaxed.

"First, has anyone in your classes ever talked about the other terrorist attacks in a way you thought was strange, like saying it was deserved, or being happy about the attacks?"

Jerry answered quickly, "Oh no, nothing like that. Most everyone is awfully upset about them. Others just don't talk about them at all."

"OK, that's good to know. Has there been anyone hanging around the campus that seemed out of place, either by dress or actions, or maybe questions?"

"Not that I can think of. Of course, it's a big place and we all seem to stick to the areas where our own classes are. There isn't much time for wandering around, but I don't know of anyone who has said anything like that. I know that would be helpful but I just don't know anything. My copter just went up and sailed around as I tested my changes in the command protocols, and the explosions only happened when I gave the command to descend. That is all I know for sure, honest!"

Tanya and I watched Jerry carefully as he spilled out what he knew, and determined that this was a gift from God. I had only one other question which I considered pretty much a waste of time but I had to ask. "Jerry, have you heard of any of the faculty talk about terrorism or the government or this country in a negative way?"

Jerry looked at me funny, but answered, "Well, some of the liberal arts Profs are, let's see how to say it, wide ranging in their thoughts. But I don't think any of them would go for this kind thing. My Profs are down to earth, no nonsense people. They talk about the math and physics of things, not political stuff like that. But then I only hear things from some friends about that sort of stuff."

"OK, I think we are about done here. Is there anything else you can think of as far as the timing of this goes?"

Jerry's father spoke up, "In all the other attacks, it's like they hate America and want to destroy it, but this is a pretty conservative state. This game always has a few nuts roaming about, but the police are pretty sharp in keeping up with those. The game is a big deal here in Alabama and people getting killed or hurt like it looks as if that was the plan was, well that would tick off a lot of diehard fans and the rest of Alabama as well. Couldn't say it wouldn't turn out ugly."

"That's what we heard and we have your plane and the controller. Can you tell me what frequency you had the controller set on?"

Jerry spoke clearly, "Yes, Sir. It was 265 megahertz. It was just a number I picked and fed into the plane and controller. It wasn't anything special, or at least I didn't think it was. I changed it from the one programmed in by the manufacturer to see if I could do it. I'm studying electrical engineering and I like to try and modify things just to see if I can, that's not illegal is it?"

"No, no." We just want to know the facts. Every little fact can or might mean the answer to who is responsible for what happened. A lot of folks don't understand the way we have to piece together bits of information to create a whole picture. We will be checking with the Stadium people as to who put the seats in, when, and then maybe we can get all the pieces to fit."

I thanked them for their cooperation and Tanya and I left. On the way back to the command area we discussed the young man and his story. "We probably should do a background check on all the professors, I doubt anything will turn up, but it has happened before, more than once. I'll call Earnest as soon as we get back to the secure communications room." Tanya nodded her agreement.

I spoke out loud my thoughts, as we drove back to the University "Tanya, I believe that we just saw another way that the Lord has intervened on the behalf of this nation. Imagine if a bomb went off in a stadium filled with a hundred thousand people! That father was right; a terrorist attack at a football game, and this one in particular, would make a lot of people mad; or at any of the other college rivalries in so many states. Oh, I know that every American is upset and angry about the other attacks, especially in Boston on Christmas Eve, but this would have been the icing on the cake to make people angrier. They are beginning to see the pattern as well."

Tanya replied, "I think you are right and I see that as a good thing. People need to know how dangerous it is becoming. Ignoring these terrorists will not protect them, because their whole idea of coming here, a western nation, is to change it."

CHAPTER 44

Roll Tide Roll?

We all gather in a conference room off of the University President's Office. We crammed into the regular seating and into folding chairs brought in to accommodate every one needed to discuss the way forward.

The University Athletic Department Lead for vendor involvement in athletic activities started the briefing by updating everyone on the specialty seats.

"Before the school year begins, we take orders for these special seats as part of the season ticket purchases. We then coordinate for vendors on the number of required cushioned seats and location in the stadium. These are comfortable but portable seats with backs and cushions that can be attached to benches in the precise seats that the attendees purchased. The vendors usually coordinate with the University's ROTC for members of the brigade to pick up the seats after the game and store them for retrieval by the vendors. It's a fund-raiser for the brigade and brought in money for special training for the cadets."

"This year, the vendors brought in the seats according to plan. The vendor told us at the beginning of the year that their normal company was under new ownership. They assured us that everything would remain in order and no one questioned the change to the company's ownership. Everything was going as normal from the beginning of the season. We were set and ready for the big game."

"Those still in storage have been checked on the off chance there were unexploded ones there. There seemed to be no pattern to the ones that exploded so we began the time consuming job of checking everyone and every possibility. The new owners supervised the replacement of the seats with special care. The seats looked like the older ones except these were a little thicker in the bottoms; the explanation was given that it would be more comfortable for the fans. No big issue, or so we thought," he ended with a wry note to his voice.

The Chief of Campus Police then spoke: "Based on our examination of unexploded seats, it seems that the bottoms were layered with some plastic explosives in the cushions. Who ever built them inserted a trigger, a small chip, into the bottom of the seats. All of them could be detonated by a radio signal from a short distance away. We are guessing the idea was to disrupt the entire game by targeting one of the most important sporting events in the country. The terrorists probably would choose when most of the fans and participants are in the stands, which we believe would have been in the first quarter right after kick off as that is usually when capacity is at the highest. This would demonstrate their power with the most casualties."

"We then began the pain-staking process of searching each area of the stadium. We brought in bomb dogs to check the rest of the seats. We took photos, dusted each seat and laying them out on the field. The bomb techs did find a small device tucked under a twisted metal rod."

The FBI bomb tech piped in, "We believe it is a remote receiver commonly used in radio controlled vehicles like cars or planes." The entire room said at once: "That's what our college student was playing with, a model plane!"

I spoke up, "Now, things are beginning to make sense. What else does someone use those things for?"

The FBI Bomb Tech remarked, "Any toy or device that runs on batteries. They even have certain 'robots' that kids play with that use this kind of receiver."

"Is there a common frequency for these controls?" I asked.

The FBI Bomb Tech replied; "Well, yes and no. Certain manufacturing companies will use one and some will use another but they are fairly common and they use a small range of frequencies for this. I would suggest you look into the company that assembled the seats and seeing if they bought them in bulk or did someone modify the seats prior to delivery or since. We are finding multiple receivers in the seats. We only had a few explode relatively speaking versus how many of these types of seats are out there. Do we know if this vendor provides seats to other colleges? Of course, we won't know for sure until we get them all separated and do an actual count.

I replied, "We have this vendor's information and DHS and the FBI are digging into their information. Right now, we'll have our 'techs' doing an internet search and the locals PD will check out all local stores that supply such things. Ok, people, I guess we have some grunt work to get on, so contact everyone you think might have info. Thanks, let's talk in two hours. We have to be able to tell the University President something about tomorrow ASAP. They are already asking, nicely now, but people come from all over to this game and we have to announce something soon. We have our crime scene investigators' testing to see what is still working and what is not. The University maintenance people are helping them."

Two hours later, we met back at the University President's Office. The meeting began with the FBI's announcement, "Based on current information and research, we are ninety percent certain that this was a planned terrorist event. Our research indicates that the new owner of the vendor company supplying the seats was a subsidiary of the Ferris Conglomerate which we now know was connected with the attack on the electrical farm located at Hoover Dam during the October 10th attacks last year. There is also an unsubstantiated connection to the foiled attack in Cleveland on the Fourth of July. We are still running this down. It has taken a long time and intense scrutiny were we able to come up with this name using our computer forensics team. We are tracking the company and found a number of 'subsidiaries' linked with it.

The room erupted with questions almost before the man finished his sentence. He held up his hand to quiet them. "We are the only ones who know this and we do not want it to become public. The quieter we keep our knowledge, the better it will for us to find the bottom of the long list of 'owners'. So, now that we have established that, the question most on the University President's mind is whether or not to go on with the game. People are flooding the town and he must make a decision.

I personally think we had a fortunate miracle from a messy and heartbreaking attack. The student inadvertently threw a monkey wrench into their plans. He caused the seats to explode early and as far as we can tell, the explosion caused little damage in the main stadium. The staff is painting over the area burned on the field and they are boarding up the damaged areas and labeling the areas as under construction. The art department professors volunteered to paint over the boards to keep the attendees from any immediate concerns. The college does all kinds of 'rah rah' things during this game so it won't cause any undue discussion except as to the content actually painted. So, this is where we stand now; we will advise President Brooks and the University President our recommendation that the game go on, unless anyone objects with the following provisions. We will place undercover officers strategically throughout the stadium, but we believe nothing will happen. The undercover officers will look for anyone leaving the game during or right after kick off and trying to make a call on a mobile device. Maybe, we can catch whoever was supposed to set them off. It is a long shot but we will try. All local and national security folks are supporting this event. Do any of you have any questions?"

A number of hands flew up and he nodded to one on the left.

"What do you think the purpose of this attack was? I haven't heard of any 'chatter' about a football game."

I replied, "In the initial manifesto by the terrorists before the 10/10 attacks, they mentioned the 'every day' parts of American life. In this season, football is about as every day as it gets. We have already had the truck bomb in Atlanta last November on Black Friday and an attempt at a mass transit attack with an improvised explosive device on the tracks in Cleveland, Ohio on the Fourth. It was prevented by an observant vet who was walking down the RTA train tracks there. He had experience with IED's in Afghanistan. He spotted what he was sure was one and notified authorities. So, we think we have touched on a possible lead and we have people checking out all leads. Keep this under the radar for now, we know the media will pick up on something happening but we are trying to keep it under wraps as much as possible, at least until we have some specific and verifiable information. I think with everyone on guard, we can safely let the game go on. We don't want a hundred thousand angry and/or scared fans on our hands over a cancelled ball game. Thank you and stay alert."

CHAPTER 45

Catching a Gator by the Tail

The game began on schedule with most of the fans unaware of what had occurred just the day before, other than a statement from the University President telling everyone about some construction damage at the stadium during a renovation project.

It all came together and agents from DHS and the FBI, along with the usual local police pulled it off with a minimum of disruption. Agents from all the agencies were strolling along the entire perimeter as well as stationed along the different access ramps throughout the stadium. They were all in civilian attire with small ear pieces that looked like the earbud's fans used to listen to the radio announcers calling the game. All the agencies agreed this would reduce the chances of creating undue concern in the fans of both teams.

About two minutes after the kickoff, I heard the agent walking the nearly empty concourse where food vendors were make a call on our internal channel, "I have a single worker acting suspicious. He had his back to the small store and he is feverishly dialing on his cell phone. He is turning, he has a frown on his face, and now is dashing out into the seating area." I could hear the roar of the crowd reached a deafening crescendo as Alabama's vaunted defense stops an Auburn first down.

The agent came back over the net, "I am following him. The noise level should cover my approach. The young man is at the center of the steps and now is clearly trying to make a call on a cell phone. He looks out on the stadium after each call. He appears to be very frustrated. I could hear multiple replies with agents converging on the agent's location. They gather at his location in less than 30 seconds. "We are leaving our mics on," they said as they approached the frustrated young man. "Sir, would you come with us?" came over the radio and we could hear the young man struggle as they each grasped an arm. The young man dropped the phone as we heard him struggling against the agents. "Sir, stop fighting!" we heard over the radio, and then after a few seconds everything quieted down as we heard them escorting him away from the crowd noise. "Sir, we are placing you in cuffs for your and our safety." was the last we heard over the net. I headed to the secure room closest to their location.

As I got to the room, they said, "He did not resist further or ask any questions. A third agent walked in and placed the dropped phone on the table which he carried in a latex gloved hand. He said, "The crowd was so focused on the game, that only those closest to the action took notice of the event and were quickly drawn back into the game. We may have no issues with what happened."

A FBI tech grab the phone, put it in an evidence bag and left the area, taking the phone to the University Security Command Post to check it out. He called over our secure net, "Yes, 265 Megahertz."

We then escorted the young man to the same command post so they could question him without the noise of the crowd and the possibility of the game ending and the normal stampede of fans creating chaos in the concourses.

I took the lead asking, "What is your name?"

"Ricky or my mother calls me Richard, Richard Wilkes. I prefer Ricky."

"Ok, Ricky, where are you from, here in Alabama?" John asked.

"No, I am from Florida but I attend school here at Alabama."

"So, what were you trying to do with your phone?" I asked.

"It was just a joke, my friend asked me to call this number right after kick off and that I would see something spectacular happen, but nothing happened." His voice was now rising as more officers arrived.

"Who is your friend?" John queried.

"Oh, his name is Mohammed," Ricky replied.

Why were you talking with Mohammed?" I took a shot in the dark.

"Some guys after class were talking about how awful life is around the University, people acting crazy, especially about football. I asked what they meant and they took me to a religious guy, to explain. I never saw them before but I was busy with school and I thought they were students too. But then, come to think of it, I haven't seen them on campus again. But the religious guy, an "Aman", I think he called himself asked me to help Mohammed play a joke to make a point during the game. I already had this job with the food vendor and he said that was perfect. All I had to do was call the preprogrammed number right after the kick off. That's all I know. Can I get back to work?"

I said in a quiet voice, "Not quite yet. Where did you talk to the Imam and what is his name?"

"I only talked with him the once and we met at a coffee shop at the Islamic Center and he just seemed like a regular guy who just dressed like the guys on TV. His name was something like Abed AL Latif, uh; he said it meant a gentle servant of the king. I thought that sounded pretty 'sick'. He got my phone number when we talked and I was surprised that he would ask me to help him make his point. He also assured me that nobody would get hurt, that it was a joke to make a point of our focus on football. I noticed that a lot of places looked different from the last game here and I thought it might be something to do with the lesson. This place does go a bit crazy for this game."

"Well, yes it does go a bit crazy but you don't know what the 'joke' was supposed to be or what the call would do?" I was watching the man closely, knowing the whole team was doing just the same.

"No, I never saw him again; another student who works in the food stands brought it to me and said nothing but to hit the redial button for the number right after kick off. I almost forgot as we were real busy until after the kick off. But they promised me a hundred dollars to do it. I can always use an extra hundred dollars."

I nodded, glanced around the officers with me who gave slight nods also. "Well, we need to know how to get in touch with you in case we have more questions and do not leave Tuscaloosa. We will want to talk with you again after you've had time to think this thing through."

"Well, I will be here until the end of the semester and then I am going home for the holidays," he said a bit belligerently. "I didn't do anything wrong!"

I held up one hand, saying, "No, you don't think you have done anything wrong but there was an attempt to do something very bad and you were at the very least a part of that. You could be charged with abetting a crime. We will have to determine if that was knowingly or as a dupe."

The young man's face paled and his mouth opened wide. Fear washed across his face and he stammered, "What do you mean?"

"I mean that this is an active investigation which we can't discuss with you at this time. Just remember that you may be needed to identify that Imam or maybe the 'students' who talked to you. It is important and we don't want you to talk about this until we have it settled. Do you understand?" I was determined to make this young man understand that this was really serious as I spoke.

"Uh, no, or maybe. Stay put and don't say anything, right?"

"You got it, now you can give this agent your contact information and he'll give you a card with a number to call if you think of anything else or see any of those people you talked with in the first place."

"Uh, yes…Sir."

I looked at the officers as they listened to the shouts of the game and the stadium roared to a crescendo.

"He is either very good or a big dupe, do a background check on him and his family in Florida and place some people to watch his residence, I don't want him to disappear like so many people have done previously."

CHAPTER 46

End Game and an Indecent Proposal?

When the game ended, I told Nick Forrest and his friend and fellow DHS agent, "You guys do a background check on the kid and his family as soon as you get back to your local office. The local police augmented by the FBI undertook the twenty-four-hour surveillance on the student and several FBI agents began a web search on the Imam. We identified an Islamic center and a Mosque in town and I asked for surveillance began on them. Now we were in the wait and see mode. Everyone, but especially the University President, was glad that the game finished with no issues and very little publicity on the explosions from the day before. The University President, who looked like he was on the edge of collapse, looked at the group and said, "I am going home, pour myself a glass of wine and retreat to my study." I smiled and replied, "I think a lot of us have the same idea."

I got the completed report on the seats later that evening. It confirmed that all the seats were fitted with a C-4 plastic explosive molded to match the seat and each one contained a small detonator that was set to respond to a 265 megahertz phone call. The explosives were covered with the usual plastic material for that type of seat and were well within the margins of size, shape, and weight of the regular foam filled seats. These seats even looked just like the seats the University had used before.

Christian and I convened the group of law enforcement people for an update. At this point no one doubted that this had been a terrorist attempt to create devastation at an American cultural event and now we had proof.

Nick Forrest and his friend shared the initial background information on the student and his family. "It seems that the young man has a reputation for liking attention and needing money. He was an easy target for this group. We cleared his family for the time being, but will continue a deeper search. Currently nothing points to anyone being radicalized in any way by any known organization.

We had the local campus law enforcement set up surveillance of the Islamic Cultural Center where the 'students' who had talked with Ricky took him. The FBI cleared all of the university personnel and no one popped up on any of the Intelligence Community chatter. The campus police captured pictures of everyone visiting the Center from the campus surveillance system and ran them against their student data base. So far, Ricky had been unable to identify any of the men who had connected him with the Imam. Ricky maintained that they didn't stand out from the student body. No long hair, turbans, beards or such and none of them struck him as Middle Eastern in looks. We had not been able to talk with the Imam from the cultural center or mosque.

So yet again, the terrorist group came close to setting another example of how close a disaster had come to America, but they were able to evaporate like the morning mist. In a few days it would be December and we felt like we were running in circles with the only break being the name of the conglomerate.

After several days in Tuscaloosa, Earnest Trowbridge called and urged us to return to Huntsville and let the rest of the federal government to continue the slow analysis following terrorist attacks. We returned to work the first Monday in December after meeting for dinner at the Summit at Redstone with the team and their families. This included Tanya who was scheduled to fly back to Washington the next day.

This was the hardest goodbye for Tanya and I so far because I proposed to her on the way to the airport in Birmingham which is where her flight was departing. I chose a restaurant for lunch and popped the question while we lingered over dessert. She was surprised but delighted to accept. We both agreed that we wanted the wedding before the end of the year. On the phone, Tanya's mother resisted for only a moment because of the short time frame to plan the wedding, but agreed to a small but elegant wedding on New Year's Eve. Everyone agreed to keep in touch and let God lead them.

CHAPTER 47

Getting Tied, but Avoiding the Dust Up

I was overwhelmed with everything happening so fast, Tanya giving me detail after detail over the phone. Her mom and her were in the final throes of preparing a New Year's Eve wedding. She even told me about how her whole family gave her a hard time about the quick wedding, but she knew by the way they acted they were rejoicing with her. In honor of the date, the wedding would be a black and white affair. Everyone except Tanya would be in black and she had found a gorgeous white dress in of all places, the American Thrift Store/Hannah Home Store. It is a large store whose income helped fund the Boy's and Girl's Clubs of Alabama. Tanya was thrilled with her purchase and that it also helped a worthy cause.

All the other men from the team and her brothers would be the groomsmen and with the exception of the maid of honor the men's wives would act as bridesmaids. Tanya's sister would be Maid of Honor. It was much bigger than either Tanya or I had wanted but we just could not deny everyone we were close to not a part of our joy.

Earnest would also be in attendance as best man for me, a secret kept by all. President Brooks and his wife weren't able to come due to the short notice and the Secret Service not being able to clear everything for his movement. Earnest told me, that all though the President wanted to attend, he wanted us to have a peaceful wedding not harangued by the local and national press. Tanya and I would be going to the White House after our honeymoon for a private celebration.

To my great surprise, Tanya had invited my first wife's parents to attend our wedding. They arrived saying that I had been the only son they ever had and that they were pleased that I was having a second chance at happiness. And besides they knew of Tanya from all her appearances on T.V. and wanted a chance to meet her.

The day was cold and sunny and all went well as everyone prepared for the ceremony. However, the oldest of Tanya's brothers brought donuts and cookies dusted with powdered sugar for the wedding party to enjoy during the process of changing clothes and getting everything ship shape.

The wedding went without any issues and several people caught a picture of my face when I first saw Tanya at the back of the church. Apparently my look of joy was an inspiration to everyone; reminding each of their own joy on their special day.

We went to a short reception and left for parts unknown, the rest of the attendees had a royal good time, but Tanya was told about the mishap and told me about it laughing as we rode in the limo.

Tanya started the story saying, "My sister went into the restroom just off the dressing room of the church and heard Becky, the bridesmaid scheduled to sing during the ceremony muttering to herself. Asking, 'What is the matter,' she was surprised to see the door to the toilet stall open and there stood Becky looking miserable, in her black dress sporting a white blob of donut icing smeared down the front of her dress, sprinkles of powdered sugar falling like snowflakes to the floor. Becky asked, "What are we going to do?"

"What am I going to do?" was my sister's reply, "I don't know what to do; you know you are dead, don't you?"

Becky moaned, "Yes, Tanya will kill me if you don't help me, PLEASE!"

So my sister replied, "OK, ok, let me think for a moment. Okay, this is what we are going to do, we will try to get as much as possible off but there will still be an ugly greasy stain on your dress. So all the rest of the bridesmaids will carry their bouquets lower than we practiced, everything will look the same and cover your spot."

Tanya continued, "They worked on the dress, using a hair dryer to dry the dress as much as possible. Then they gathered all the bridesmaids in the bathroom to share the change in where they would carry their bouquets with them. A bit of disagreement took place but it was decided that they would do this for one of their own. The singer stayed as far from Tanya as possible."

"But Becky still had a problem, what was she to do when she had to sing. My sister informed her that she would just have to carry the bouquet up with her while she sang. Poor Becky just hung her head and nodded.

Fortunately, no other issues arose to take away from the beautiful ceremony and I thought it was funny. They all love us so much; they didn't want anything to spoil our day."

CHAPTER 48

The Look for His Missing Operative

It was February before anything else happened. It was about the time we expected someone to come looking for Pandya. In Houston our long vigil was rewarded although we did not realize it at first. The surveillance team took the picture of a man who walked in with his head held high and making no attempt to hide his face. We noted as he turned to look back that he had a vicious scar that cut down one half of his face.

Mean while, Fletcher Cordell spoke with everyone at the Mosque. None of them knew anything about where Charles was located. The Imam only said, "Charles left alone one evening about five months ago and I have not heard from him, nor have I heard anything about his vehicle. I did not expect to hear from him again, since you were sending him away. I assumed he'd reached his destination and was on his way to his next assignment."

Fletcher Cordell, concerned with the lack of information on Charles, who was instrumental in setting the ground work for all the attacks on this arrogant country, decided to check again with the points of contact Charles should have met along the way to see if there was any recent sighting of him. Since he had more fish to fry, he arranged to leave the country using a 'coyote' to get him through the tunnels used to smuggle people into the U.S. The 'coyote' happy to have a paying customer going the other way quickly made the necessary arrangements.

Cordell left the Mosque late in the night by a side entrance hoping he could slip out of the country without being seen. He thought he was a ghostly shadow in the dark of night. Unbeknownst to him, the surveillance team trailed him from the mosque to his link up point with the coyote.

By the next afternoon, he had reached Mexico City and boldly took a flight to Cordova, Spain. With the disappearance of his protégée, he didn't want to take any chances by remaining in the US. He was done with the United States for a while. He had shown them the power of Allah. He was proud of his people, and although they had lost a few people along the way that was the nature of war, a war he knew Allah would make sure they won.

CHAPTER 49

Closing the Intelligence Loop and a Pregnant Pause

The surveillance team sent the picture of Fletcher to us, just like all the other pictures taken. Earnest, having read my report of the interviews with Pandya, noted the scar. He called me, and I arrived the next day. He agreed that this person just might be the man their prisoner described.

Carrying the picture, I walked into Tumbrel Pandya's cell. He was sitting in the small cell, only let out to exercise in the hallway twice a day. He was startled to hear the door being unlocked. He almost smiled when he saw me walk into his cell. "Ah, what an unexpected visit. I was not expecting company today, let me clear my calendar for you, since I am bored with my normal visitors. You can give me a break in the normal tedium of my isolation."

I smiled back and said, "We have a picture of someone we think you might know and we'd like to see if we are correct." I handed the enlarged picture to him.

Pandya hand shook slightly and his pupils dilated as he gazed upon the picture of the man who had won his heart to the cause of Islamic rule of the world. I didn't even ask if he recognized him, the reaction was clear to me.

"Where was he?" He muttered under his breath.

"Entering the Mosque you left in Houston, we are checking him out now."

"Well, I doubt it will do you any good, he is the best of us." Pandya said.

"Well thanks anyway. You will be moved to another prison soon and I doubt I will see you again. It has certainly been interesting." *"Assalamu 'Alaikum"*.

Pandya looked down speaking in a low surprised tone, "And '*Wa'alaikum Assalam*' to you as well."

I briefed Earnest about my meeting and he told me the following: "After all the information your team has gathered, the President is making the following decisions with the Department of Homeland Security. We have issued orders to have the State Department freeze all the assets of any company in which they were able to link to the Ferris Conglomerate. They also put the picture of the scarred visitor, aka Fletcher Cordell, on the FBI's Most Wanted List and sent it to all the law enforcement agencies around the world. They also put it on the news as a person of interest in a murder investigation and sent it to every intelligence agency around the world." I flew back to Huntsville after leaving Earnest's office that evening.

Thus, by the time I was ready to leave the mosque in Cordova, Spain, my picture was on the front page of every newspaper and my credit cards and sources of money were frozen. The Imam in the mosque sequestered me immediately and began a frantic plan to smuggle me back to Afghanistan as quickly as possible. I had risen to number one on the international wanted list just as Osama bin Laden had been for years.

I arrived home to my new wife who had her own good news. Tanya gave me a hug and said, "You are looking at the newest employee with the AMC Public Affairs and Congressional office and I wanted to welcome daddy home." I didn't catch the last part at first. I said, "Congratulations on getting a job here." Then the second part of her statement hit me hard. "What did you say?" "I said I got a job with PAO." "I heard that, what else did you say?" I said welcome home daddy!" I sputtered, "You'rr pregnant? How did that happen?" Laughing, she said, "Well, did your parents tell you about the birds and the bees?" I blushed and we started laughing. We were starting to settle down to a normal life, but of course, we along with the rest of the team, would remain in-touch with the Chief of Staff and the President, as she was still the public face of the 10/10 attacks.

Meanwhile, my life with Tanya became a celebration of joy every day. We had our serious moments but also lots of laughter and peace in our marriage. I continued to marvel at my second chance of true love, thanking the Lord over and over. I was also pleased that Tanya chose to remain in contact with my late wife's parents. Now, since Tanya had shared the news with me that morning that we were soon to be parents, they too would be able to rejoice in a grandchild. She had caused my joy to explode by telling me that she would let them know along with my and her families. She was a continual source of joy and comfort to me! She also really enjoyed working with the media outlet for AMC and continued to help when asked by Earnest Trowbridge.

CHAPTER 50

The Comedy of Errors, Celebrity Life and Presidential Politics

We spoke with President Brooks and Earnest the next morning. I told them, "Again, we continue to review the Ferris Construction Company or Conglomerate. When we contacted the company that supplied the special seats, they claimed no knowledge about the buyer beyond the lawyer who had approached them to buy the company. They gave us the name of the lawyer and the law firm responsible for the sale. It was located in Minneapolis, Minnesota but when we had the local authorities check it out, the lawyer and the law firm were gone. Supposedly it had sold the company during the summer. No fingerprints or pictures were available at the company, which follows a pattern we have seen before."

"Nick did a quick check with INS (Immigration and Naturalization Service), and we can now confirm that the tunnel our suspect used to escape is a known route used by 'coyotes' to bring people over the border. INS is not used to watching anyone traveling in the opposite direction and so do not often monitor it 24/7. This comes as no surprise, but we still grumbled at the continued lack of a secure border."

We tested ever scenario we could regard as possible to determine what had happened, who was behind it, and just what would be next. It is nerve racking to say the least. There have been several small attacks off and on but the local police determined them to be 'lone wolf' in nature and most of the perps died at the scene. Those perps captured by the police didn't say anything that didn't sound like rehearsed talking points from extremist web sites."

Life in the United States slowly returned to the mush of daily celebrity nonsense and now, a Presidential race. The attacks were the stuff of ads and counter ads; everyone reached their saturation point quickly. We still studied all the intelligence on a regular basis, but couldn't develop any new leads.

Tumbrel Pandya was quietly transferred to the Guantanamo Bay prison and forgotten by everyone but me. My new walk with the Lord caused me be concerned about the young man's fatalistic view that he would be killed as a matter of fact. I prayed for Tumbrel to learn the truth of Jesus and come to a faith in Christ.

During the months that followed, I wrote Tumbrel several letters expressing my appreciation for his dedication to his beliefs but that I was concerned with his lack of hope for a future. I explained some of my own struggles after my late wife's untimely death and now my joy in a new family. I simply told him of my sincere belief that Jesus had orchestrated a whole new life for me. After a few letters, I was thrilled to hear from Tumbrel that he was thinking of all I had shared with him. I began to plan a trip to see him after all the paperwork could be worked out. Tanya was an eager participant in the letters and the planned visit.

CHAPTER 51

The Training of Death, Destruction and Mayhem

After a tortuous trip via the smaller Mosques from Spain to Afghanistan, I, Majid te Aziz, aka. Fletcher Cordell, arrived near my old home in the mountains. The long trip did allow me to speak with many Imams across southern Spain, Morocco, Algeria, Tunisia, Libya, Egypt, Saudi Arabia, and Iran. This enlarged my network of contacts considerably.

I received a quiet welcome as a conquering hero at each location along my path by those who knew anything about my activities. But the number of people knowing my true identity was kept very small, most only knowing that I had been in the United States during a number of successful attacks. It was enough for them.

I knew satellite surveillance was able to track even small gatherings in the areas know to be terrorist strongholds. No one wanted an attack by the pesky drones used by the allies in the war on terrorism to keep the war sanitary.

I decided to take this time to rest and regroup, having lost my anonymity on the world stage. My scar marked me, making me unable to travel openly anymore, but my communication network was in great condition. I would work to build it even larger and more diverse. I now had operatives in virtually every area of the world and perhaps I would soon be able to order the attacks from my mountain stronghold like Osama Bin Laden.

As I met with the leadership in the area, I quizzed each about their men. I was especially interested in some of the younger men who I could train to be facilitators as I myself had done for so many years. I could no longer travel because of my exposure to the world. But there would be a young man who was canny and able to learn quickly. And I rejoiced that my contact stream was now so much larger making communications much easier and less vulnerable to being tracked by our enemies.

In the end there were three men I was personally watching as they reacted to various situations. I purposely sent them on short missions with trained observers to test each of them. There could be no display of anger or reaction when things did not pan out according to plan plus an ability to blend in with various cultural styles. I could not instill this in them; it would have to be a natural part of their personalities as it had been for me. And no deformities to make them easily identified. I would love to have another Pandya, looking western and yet sold out to Allah. Allah would provide and guide me and my effort, of this I was certain.

After a long month of testing, I felt I had found my men; deciding that Allah had given me three men to act according to the standards set for me when I began. The men were from three different areas of Pakistan and Afghanistan and each showed an aptitude for languages, different languages and different skills for each of them. This way I could be active in more than one area around the world at the same time. I saw this as a gift from Allah for the speeding up of the coming of the 'Mahdi' the final Imam prophesied by the Quran.

After the men began their long training preparing them for their missions, I spent much time in prayer preparing to make my own 'hajj' journey to Mecca. Because of my scar, normal travel arrangements were out of the question. But, traveling by stealth the way I had come home was still available to me. I could still move through the Muslim countries using private vehicles and wearing the traditional head gear which could hang down across one side of my face when I was somewhat in the open. After years of traveling around the world but especially in the United States, I was finally in a position to make this journey. The requirements for this journey were that I had to be in a financial position to take care of my family while being gone. I had no family left but had been offered the daughter of one of the local leaders as a wife. I was seriously considering it since I could no longer travel alone. My bride and I could make the journey together as another way to disguise my identity.

After a month of preparation, the marriage took place in the bride's home village performed by the local Imam. It was quiet and joyous for my bride and her family as they felt blessed to be marrying a true soldier for Allah. I was calm and authoritative in taking a wife. She would offer me extra cover and I was happy to have a wife of good background. I was not enamored with her but she was shy, pretty, and quiet, the perfect mate in my eyes. She made no demands on my time and seemed content to meet my needs in every way.

I took up the last of the training for my three protégé's when we returned home after the wedding ceremony. This was the training them on how to be a 'ghost', the area I had personally perfected over the years.

My three students had been in the fight since joining as teenagers. 'Adab', meaning one with good manners was slated for the west, the U. S., Canada, and Mexico. 'Basirah' whose name means 'one with deep knowledge, insight, perceptive with discernment was going to the European area of the battlefield. Last but definitely not least, was 'Qurhah' whose name means 'close to God' would be his Middle Eastern and Far Eastern facilitator.

I considered the western nations the most difficult to deal with for my purposes. Each of these men could fill in any where I needed them to after their intensive training, modeled after the one I had gone through. I was feeling good about the future; Allah was blessing me greatly.

CHAPTER 52

The Irony of Capture

As the months went by, the men I had chosen to replace me in the field were as ready as I could make them. They had studied as I had, maps, languages, the way I had done things, the way I wanted them done. So, I began the process of sending them out around the world to the places I designated for each of them. Satisfied that I had done all I could, I sent them forth with a special blessing from the local Imam and myself.

Now, I could turn my attention to my new wife and our Hajj to Mecca. The local Imam made our arrangements to travel by private vehicles back through the route I had taken coming back to Afghanistan. It was circuitous and slow but I felt we had plenty of time and the people in each country were glad to be of assistance. They too had seen or heard of the media touting my place as the now leading terrorist on the kill list by the west. They saw it as an honor to help me in this most important journey for any Muslim.

We left a month before the time of Hajj and were traveling through so many countries but never with a passport or identification. We arrived in al-Basra, Iraq after a long ride through Iran having crossed into Iran from Afghanistan. This small area nestled between Iran and Kuwait, was a major port in the area and the port designated as the one from which Sinbad the Sailor had departed. The area had been the scene of some of the heaviest fighting from March to May 2003 during the invasion of Iraq by the Allied Forces.

As we traveled, we spent the night at homes along the way and now in the town, my wife wanted to buy some fresh fruit at the market. So, we stopped at the market and she went forth with just the driver as I waited in the car.

Within moments, I heard a loud explosion from inside the oldest market in Basra, a place where dissidents of both the Sunnis and Kurds held a level of sway and I jumped out of the car to check it out. I ran toward the sounds of screaming and wails to find the place destroyed by a bomb. I asked quickly what had happened and was informed that a suicide bomber had just blown himself up at the most prominent fruit stand in the market.

I stood in shock for a moment then began a studied search for my wife and driver. I strode through the whole market with no sign of either. When asked, a policeman informed me that a woman and two men had died in the attack.

I shook my head, aware of how many times I had ordered this type of attack and sensing that I had just experienced it from the other side of the coin. I wasn't heartbroken but I did acknowledge the irony of my wife dying in such an attack.

A senior police officer arrived and took me into custody as well as almost every other male in the area. I had let my face be fully seen in my rush. The local police took me to the jail and reported the incident to the Iraqi Forces in the area.

After being put into a cell and my picture taken, I knew it would be the end of my jihad.

EPILOGUE

Evil Goes Into Hiding

On a late Friday night, simultaneous raids by the FBI and ATF at the main Mosques identified by their intelligence source, Tumbrel Pandya, as being key supporters of the various attacks from 10/10 to Disneyland took place. Pandya having finally broken during my visit to him in Guantanamo, shared with me key personnel involved at each location. The raid teams picked them up as they were leaving their respective Mosques. Even the Imams who had been instrumental in making arrangements were taken into custody including those from Minneapolis, St. Louis, and Houston.

The FBI avoided entering the individual Mosques in order to avoid unwanted publicity. They captured each person independently away from their Mosques. This created confusion in the local communities because the men just disappeared. The arrest teams took extreme caution to avoid a repeat of the mess in Iowa where the number of men in the compound far exceeded the number expected causing the loss of agents from both services. The Federal Agencies had watched the three places for several months and even a CI (confidential informant) had gone to several

Friday prayer services at each one. Thus a large number of men were picked up quietly and swiftly.

They were whisked into private holding areas for individual interrogations. After months of interrogation some fruitful, but most just confirming what the we already knew, they were shipped to Guantanamo, joining Pandya. We made sure he was never seen by any of them as they were each held in isolation and only allowed out for exercise individually.

We were all there for the massive interrogations. The Imams were the most difficult demanding rights and lawyers only to be told just what Pandya had been told. They were being held under the Patriot's Act and therefore would not be given access to lawyers and such. Most remained quiet for a month or so, but then grew restless in their isolation from each other and the world.

With the arrests complete, we kept video surveillance set up on properties in the areas surrounding the Mosques so all three were under continual surveillance monitoring the comings and goings around them. There were no sightings of our main target but all personnel involved in this quest continued to look for possible new people visiting the Mosques.

I and the others felt that our target was intelligent and must have felt the noose tightening and decided to have new people come to the Imams. Or was he laying low like Osama Bin Laden had prior to his final date with American Seals.

Only later did the CoS learn through back channels of the disappearance of our main target. This raised a few eyebrows and questions around our celebratory table. His arrest in Iraq appeared to disappear with no records available. Fletcher was never heard from again, he just disappeared off the face of the earth. The impounded vehicle turned to rust in the desert police compound, never claimed. No one ever spoke of the incident again. Silence surrounded both the bomb blast and the famous captive. All that was known for sure was that our target had disappeared into the hands of the Iraqi and Allied Forces. There remained questions in our minds but at least we knew that news from Earnest was good news.

This part of our quest appeared complete and we were only left with the question of whether that man had trained others that we did not know to take his place.

Therefore, the team remained vigilant despite the quiet following the raids. The world and the country as a whole slowly forgot the attacks and seeped back into a complacent normalcy.

The team of John Banks, Christian Blade, Dan Griffin, Bill Marks, Marcus Owens, Jeremy Hunt, and Tanya Banks remained in anonymity only praised by Earnest and the President.

We took as our verse: 1 Peter 5:8-9 "Be alert and of sober mind. Your enemy the devil prowls around like a roaring lion looking for someone to devour. Resist him, standing firm in the faith, because you know that the family of believers throughout the world is undergoing the same kind of sufferings" ...

CPSIA information can be obtained
at www.ICGtesting.com
Printed in the USA
BVHW031921190822
645022BV00013B/179

9 781662 826672